All the Little Wars

By the same author

At the Chelsea

All the Little Wars

BY
FLORENCE TURNER

HAMISH HAMILTON · LONDON

HAMISH HAMILTON · LONDON
HAMISH HAMILTON LTD

Penguin Books Ltd, 27 Wrights Lane, London W8 5TZ (Publishing & Editorial)
and Harmondsworth, Middlesex, England (Distribution & Warehouse)
Viking Penguin Inc., 40 West 23rd Street, New York, New York 10010, U.S.A.
Penguin Books Australia Ltd, Ringwood, Victoria, Australia
Penguin Books Canada Limited, 2801 John Street, Markham, Ontario, Canada L3R 1B4
Penguin Books (N.Z.) Ltd, 182–190 Wairau Road, Auckland 10, New Zealand

First published in Great Britain 1987 by
Hamish Hamilton Ltd
Copyright © 1987 by Florence Turner

British Library Cataloguing-in-Publication Data

Turner, Florence
All the little wars.
I. Title
823'.914 [F]   PR6070.U714/
ISBN 0-241-12425-5

Set in 11/13pt Baskerville by Butler & Tanner Ltd
Printed and bound in Great Britain by
Butler & Tanner Ltd, Frome and London

To Ian Le Maistre

Contents

Of these stories, LOW ALTAR, THE HANGING MAN, PERILOUS SEAS and INCIDENT AT LIMA JUNCTION have been broadcast on BBC Radio 3. THE FEDERAL AGENTS ARE COMING was published by *Vogue*; STAG LINE and PERILOUS SEAS by *Woman's Journal*; THIS IS MY MISTRESS by *Eastern World*; MRS HASSETT'S HOLIDAY by *El Quixote*, THE DARK GODS won the Scottish Arts Council Short Story Award of 1982 and was published in a collection by Collins.

Low Altar

Walking home from the bank for lunch, Julian noticed that the durian tree at the bottom of the driveway had begun to drop its fruit. The big, prickly purple globes lay in the coarse grass, but he knew they would not be there for long. The addicts would find them soon: Miss Veitch, the bony Scottish nurse who lived next door; or Julian's syce, Said, or any random Malay who happened to pass that way.

'When the durian falls the penis rises.'

Thus ran the Malayan couplet. He had heard it sung at a *ronggeng* where men danced with men because it was considered incorrect for a Malay woman to dance in public unless she were a prostitute; Julian had danced. His partner was a very young man with hair dyed an improbable shade of red. He wore heavy make-up and smiled beguilingly and with a knowledge of what could be. Julian's friends had laughed and egged him on with lacivious smirks. His wife Deirdre had condoned it. Everyone had been drunk. Julian had suddenly stopped dancing, unable to explain it was sadness and not disgust that prevented him continuing.

Durian, it was said, acted as an aphrodisiac. Few Europeans tried it. The pulpy, slimy fruit tasted obnoxiously of sherry and rotting meat; sugar, garlic and a foetid something more like a smell than a taste. After eating it, Julian knew from experience, the breath was foul. Yet there were addicts. Maggie Veitch, the nurse, if already started on her compulsion, would remain incommunicado for several days, knowing she was, as she herself put it, long face stricken with a smile, 'too pongy for decent company'.

Deirdre was waiting for Julian in the living room of their

low, wide-windowed bungalow. At least he hoped she was
waiting for him. She sat beautifully at one end of the long,
chintz-covered couch, bare legs crossed at the ankles. She wore
a sleeveless, rose-coloured linen dress and looked elegantly cool
under the whirling teak ceiling fan.

As Julian kissed her, he guessed she had not been thinking of
him at all. She had not been waiting.

'Darling.'

They spoke together, the mutual endearment tinged with
differing shades of feeling, his warm, hers automatic.

'The durians are beginning to fall,' he said.

'Oh, God, I suppose Said will start eating them. It'll be worse
than the Singapore River.'

'Nothing smells worse than the Singapore River.'

Julian was watching his wife. How lovely she was. Yet there
was this distance between them. Last night! It must be because
of last night. He should have yielded to her wish that the light
remain on. She wanted to look at them together, she said. When
he hesitated, she had fallen silent, removing herself from him,
though she remained on the bed. It was exactly what she
wanted to see, the urgency of his manhood, that embarrassed
him. How could she like him in such an aggressively physical
state? Lovemaking should be gentle, private, in the dark. It
was more exciting that way.

'Captain Fourscu telephoned,' she said.

'Oh, marvellous.'

Julian enjoyed their Danish friend. He and Deirdre had met
him when they had taken a trip to Java the previous year.
Fourscu's 300-ton freighter plied between Java and Bangkok,
carrying cargo and occasionally a few passengers. He was
bearded, forthright and middle-aged (they thought of him as
old, being themselves in their twenties), and his sea-captain's
blue eyes watched the world with amusement.

'I asked him for a drink,' she said, looking animated now, as
she always did when concerned with pleasure. Good times, as
she put it. Julian's own pleasure mitigated the guilt he felt at

not yet having given her a child. Only occasionally did he consider that it was not altogether his fault.

'Rich will want to see him,' he said.

Rich was their closest friend. A Welsh meteorologist, he formed the protective triumvirate of two males and a female. In Singapore, in this year of 1938, the ratio of men to women was necessarily far greater than two to three. And Deirdre's beauty was of the obvious kind.

'Oh, he's bound to turn up during the evening. Captain Fourscu has probably given him a ring already.' She sounded uninterested. He wondered why.

The heat was crushing as he left the house to return to his office. It was probably foolhardy to walk, but he enjoyed the small dramas he passed. Working in a bank paid well, but it was stifling. Now, pausing near the Chinese graveyard where old tombstones slumped against one another, he watched two Chinese airing their caged birds on the grassy verge. As he did, a small open sports car smashed by, disappearing up the drive leading to Julian's house. Julian recognised the driver's dark curls. Rich! The bugger could have given him a wave. Perhaps he hadn't noticed. Julian walked on. Some obscure notion of keeping fit must be the reason for this inane activity during the hottest part of the day. He did not play cricket, indeed, apart from dancing and some rather indifferent swimming, Julian took no exercise. He was tall, with a long, slender torso. His black hair lay smoothly against his skull; he had a sallow skin and deep-set, intelligent eyes. He liked people, but was shy, looking over shoulders when introduced, dropping hands after a brief pressure. Though not as popular as Deirdre, people admired him and said he would 'go far'. He had, after all, received a double first at Cambridge.

That night, Captain Fourscu, all portly stomach and good will, took them to dinner at a Chinese restaurant and then to the Happy World, a big amusement park and dancehall. Julian, already a little drunk, followed his wife and Fourscu through the boisterous crowds, past shooting galleries and sideshows

and into the dancehall where a band of Filipino musicians
played vaguely Hawaiian-sounding music in a jazz tempo.
Against the walls sat rows of taxi girls, chaperoned by their
mothers.

'I dance with you,' announced the Captain, and led Deirdre
to the floor. Julian ordered a gin and tonic and sat damply
alone at a table by the dancefloor. The taxi girls looked like
rows of tulips. One wore a red dress with no straps. Her skin
was like thick cream. Probably a Eurasian, he thought. He
wished he could remove his jacket, but it was not done.
At home, Julian wore a sarong in the evening. To him, it
was the most elegant of costumes as well as the coolest. When
people suggested by their comments that this habit was less
an eccentricity than a perversion, Julian shrugged. He did
not care what people thought, except possibly the Malays
who would not, perhaps, approve, considering it to be a cheap
Western simulation. Yet Julian believed that the Malays,
gentle people as they were, would not give a damn how he
dressed.

Aware he was growing quite drunk, Julian did not articulate
his thoughts. To do so would have brought him squarely up
against the reason for being drunk in the first place. Why had
Deirdre not mentioned that Rich had been to see her?

He continued to stare at the taxi dancers. The wild effluvium
of the tropical night made him suddenly dizzy. Perfume and
drying rubber; spices and Indian *ghee*; ten times over the Singapore River; there was no end to the smells. Or the sounds,
for that matter. Tinkle and clash and whine; slow drumming;
the cackle of old *amahs* and the strange cries of the street vendors.
The girl in red was dancing now. Julian watched her undulate.
He felt desire, wanting to plunge into all the warm, palpitating
flesh around him pulling it close, burying his face in the dark,
in the dark . . .

'When the durian falls the penis rises,' he quoted aloud.

'Talking to yourself? Bad sign.'

It was Rich. His curls were taut; so was his body. Nothing

sagged, nothing was limp. Heavy black brows nearly met over dark brown eyes. There was a merry sexuality about him. Julian glowered, feeling tired and skinny. He was pleased to remember Rich had red hair under one armpit, black under the other.

'Not dancing?'

'I'm waiting for your wife to be free. Isn't that old Fourscu?'

'You know it is. Who else looks like a fat, middle-aged Dane?'

Why did Rich bother to lie? Deirdre would have told him about the Captain.

The music eased off. A girl in a white, bouffant dress (Chinese? Malay? mixed?—he did not care) began to sing in a shrill voice.

'*Terang boelan*—The moon is full . . .'

The captain and Deirdre returned. Deirdre said 'hello' coolly to Rich but Captain Fourscu announced loudly his pleasure at meeting 'my friend'.

'Is goot. And now you will come with us to Bangkok.'

'Bangkok?' asked Julian. 'What do you mean?'

Deirdre replied, 'Captain Fourscu has invited us to go to Bangkok with him next week. On his freighter.'

She tacked on the last remark absent-mindedly. Julian noticed she was watching Rich. A moment later they left to dance.

'Don't show it.' Julian glanced around, startled.

'You must not show it,' said the Captain again. 'She cannot help that she is beautiful, and that there are not many European women around. Of course that does not matter to me.' He laughed. 'I tell you what we do.'

In the end Julian agreed to invite Maggie Veitch who accepted in a pleased way, assuring Julian her durian orgy was over.

But when they went on board the ship—*Den Klare Stjerne*, The Evening Star—on the day arranged, the passenger list had risen to six. A honeymoon couple, Major and Mrs. Cameron Rogers were taking the trip.

'But he's ADC to the General Officer in Command.' Julian

sounded offended. 'The GOC's son too. They're Plymouth Brethren.'

Captain Fourscu looked amused. 'We still will drink our *schnapps* when the sun is over the yardarm.'

The honeymooners were the last to arrive. Major Rogers was slight and very straight. His brown hair was cut close in military style. Mrs. Rogers appeared to fall up the gangplank. But it was illusory. She was much taller than her husband with long, thin legs that scrambled. She carried a huge woven basket and her face was hidden by a wide-brimmed hat.

The ship's whistle blasted; they were on their way. Singapore gradually became a bruise on the horizon, then vanished.

'Jolly decent of you to give us your cabin.'

This was said to Julian over pre-dinner drinks, served by the Captain. It was one of the few remarks they were to hear from Cameron Rogers. He and his bride maintained their privacy to the point of ostentation. The other passengers, who slept on deck, save for Maggie Veitch who was given the single cabin, respected it.

Den Klare Stjerne had wide decks divided by the cabin section and the dining room. Rich slept on one deck, Julian and Deirdre on the other. Sleeping on deck was for Julian an experience of sensuality. The dull drumbeat of the ship's engines was forgotten below enormous stars, or the mad, swollen beauty of the moon on the third day. Flying fish skipped over the silver water and beside him Deirdre's half-naked body lay in the quicksilver light. He wanted her: this semi-dark ambiance excited him. But from the first night, it was her turn to say, 'No, not here. It's too public.'

Humiliated, he lay sleepless and was still awake at sunrise. The ship's engines had stopped and he sat up to see they were lying off shore. The scent of land and flowers and the salt air drove him to the railing. For a moment he was Conrad.

Below, a rowing boat, heavily laden, approached. Siamese vendors scurried up the rope ladder and presently a lively bargaining began on the forward deck as the ship's Chinese cook purchased vegetables, rice and a black piglet.

As he watched, Julian head a soft voice: 'The poor little beast. I dare say we will eat him.'

It was Mrs. Rogers. She wore a white blouse and her legs were covered to the knees by loose, ugly white shorts.

'I dare say. Do you like pork?'

She looked at him gravely from pale blue eyes. Her sandy hair was cut short and parted neatly on one side.

'I'm afraid I do.'

Abruptly she walked away. Behind him, Julian heard Deirdre stirring on their mattress. Through a yawn she said 'Wasn't that the bride? She's up rather early.'

He did not reply, disliking the innuendo. Yesterday, he had heard the large, genial mate, Janssen, laying bets with Rich as to how many times Major Rogers would achieve satisfaction with his wife. How bloody crude! Yet, perversely, he wondered himself how it would be to lie with that thin, pale body.

During the next few days, in gentle weather, Julian fished over the side of the ship whenever Fourscu stopped to let the others go swimming or chip oysters off the rocks of outlying islands. He found the sport soothing. Strange things came from the purple-green tropical waters, less like fish than excrescences of the sea. Some were ruby-eyed, some yellow; now and then a sad eye flickered. He knew none by name and threw them all back into their shadowed environment.

Fishing also helped him ignore the growing closeness between his wife and Rich on their return from swimming and oyster excursions. Deirdre was burned gold by the sun; her chestnut hair turned tawny. A wonderful pair, thought Julian, and suppressed his pain, keeping more and more to his side of the double mattress.

Young pork had been served in various disguises three times before the ship reached its first Siamese port. It was a mere village with a central muddy street, *atap* huts on stilts and more pigs wandering hopefully. As always, stench and flower fragrance mingled.

They did not go ashore until next morning. The Captain announced at breakfast an intended visit to a temple. It was not too bad a walk through jungle and they would find it interesting.

Julian, who had slept badly, followed Deirdre down the gangway. Her full, flowered, *dirndl* skirt twitched on her hips. A white peasant blouse left her shoulders bare. At the bottom of the gangway, she slipped and was caught and briefly held by Rich who waited on the jetty. Deirdre laughed and turned her head towards Julian, though he knew she did not see him. Any moment, he thought, they would start holding hands.

The wedding couple was late. When they arrived, Julian heard Rich begin a laugh, quickly quelled. Angry, he looked up to see Mrs. Rogers moving down to the jetty. She wore a leopard-patterned bathing suit with a matching parasol. It was a travesty of fashion, but somehow innocent. Julian, embarrassed, stared groundwards. Mrs. Cameron's big toes were long, seeming not to fit her white sandals.

Captain Fourscu's mood was martial. He manipulated his passengers until presently, stared at by small children, they walked single-file along a muddy path through the village. It led them finally into an insect-loud jungle where they sweated and swept banana leaves against the greedy flies. Only Cameron Rogers carried a regulation fly whisk of horsehair on a stick.

'Is not long,' comforted the Captain.

Maggie Veitch, big breasts flopping, led the way. She strode on mud-splattered tennis shoes, her laughter hearty in the tropical shade-and-sunlight. Everything to her seemed an adventure, endorsed by need and common sense. It was this, Julian reflected, mopping sweat from his eyes, that allowed her to indulge in durian orgies. She could get drunk on vintage champagne and not even know its worth, thought Julian, plucking at something prickling his neck. Perhaps there was something splendidly honest about all this.

The prickling turned out to be a large red ant, the kind known as *keringa*. He threw it away, but not before it had badly stung him. He swore and rubbed the painful spot.

Behind him, Mrs. Cameron: 'What happened?'

'It's nothing,' but he held out his hand for her to see. Looking at her in her leopard-skin made him think of Le Douanier Rousseau. Her husband, however, hovering near, was less than Le Douanier Rousseau—a clockwork soldier, momentarily human. His narrow brow wrinkled in concern.

'Better get that seen to.'

'Oh, it's nothing.' Julian felt ridiculous.

Mrs. Rogers had dropped his hand quickly. Raising her parasol again she set off on long legs, stepping high. Her husband, offering Julian a small salute, followed, horsehair whisking busily.

'What happened?'

Deirdre had dropped back to walk with him.

'Nothing, Just an insect bite.'

'Oh.' She seemed satisfied and walked on ahead once more. Julian noticed that Rich waited for her.

Their path took them now into a jungle gloom. Light fell lancelike through the heavy trees. At times they trod on the softness of moss. Monkeys shouted, and a jumbled hum of insect voices sounded around and above, blocking thought. It grew hotter. Julian felt the beginnings of a heat rash between his legs. At the head of the line, the Captain called out again, 'Not long now'.

The pattern of their walk had changed. They no longer moved in single file and the path was wider now. Julian walked next to Captain Fourscu; the Rogers were side by side but did not touch; Deirdre had fallen back. Glancing round, Julian saw that indeed she and Rich were holding hands. He felt pinched and sad.

Abruptly they were in a clearing. Pausing, Julian sensed Deirdre close behind. He smelled her, a muskily sweet mixture of woman and *Tabac Blanc*, an expensive perfume he had given her for Christmas. He had given her many gifts, including himself, if he could be considered a gift.

'We are here,' the Captain informed them.

At the far side of the clearing stood a temple, small, inde-
terminate, built of stone corroded now by heat and rain and
white ants. Curiously, no one spoke. An atavistic silence held
them, and they stayed where they were, wonderingly, like
frozen statues, as in the game children play.

The Captain ravished their silence. 'It is to this place the
women come. Many of them, hey Bruno?'

The mate nodded. 'Many.' His tone fell to a hushed version
of awe. Behind it lay a snicker. 'They bring their offerings.' He
winked at the Captain. 'The ladies should not see, perhaps.'

'Don't be silly.' Deirdre sounded excited. 'Of course we want
to see.'

Julian eyed her tiredly. 'We?' he thought and glanced at
Mrs. Rogers who had perched herself on one of two big fallen
rubber tree trunks, cut down to help make the clearing. They
lay across one another, peeled of bark, white and smooth. Julian
looked at them again, his breath held, then escaping in a gasp.
The trunks had been painstakingly carved at their tips into
perfect artifacts of the human penis: a giant titivation for the
gods.

Mrs. Rogers did not appear to have noticed; nor had, as yet,
anyone else, save Captain Fourscu and the mate, who were
grinning.

After a moment, Maggie Veitch said, 'Who's for going in?'

She aimed her fist at the mate's chest, but withheld it just
before contact. Her voice was coarse, threaded with double
meaning. Activated by durians, thought Julian, and deliberately kept his gaze from the trunk-endings. Then he saw Mrs.
Rogers staring at them. She knew, and understood. Freckles
showed lividly through the pallor of her skin.

'It is a temple of fertility,' the mate was saying in the tones
of a travel guide. 'The women come hoping to please the god
of love. They hope their ... offerings will give potency to their
husbands, and fertility to themselves.'

The snicker was still there.

'Oh!' It was a screech from Maggie Veitch, a yap of prudent joy. She was pointing at the tree trunks. 'Look, oh, I say, would you believe it?'

All of them looked now. Mrs. Rogers turned away and stared at her husband who stood with his fly-swich dangling loosely. Julian felt a vast boredom. He drew his fingers swiftly down the smooth surface of the top trunk, then turned and walked straight into the dark, incense-smelling interior of the temple. In a moment, everyone had followed. The gigglings and pointings dwindled in the face of what they saw and finally absorbed on the low altar before them. It was piled deep with phalluses carved from wood. They were all lengths, all thicknesses, wrought with skill and meaning. Their mere quality silenced the visitors. Julian imagined the women, softly walking in their bright sarongs, hope in their hands, a carefully carved supplication to forgive their inabilities. Or was it the inability of their men?

He turned away, brushing past Rich who sent him a quick smile at the same time dropping his hand from Deirdre's shoulder. Julian ignored them both. He wanted nothing more than to get back to the ship.

That evening, much drink was consumed. A local rubber-planter and his wife had been invited aboard, and the cook had made a many-dished *rijstafel*. As the meal ended, Julian left the steamy dining room, murmuring excuses. He went on deck. The air felt sweet against his face. He looked up and his head swam with starlight. In the cabin, someone must have been telling a story, for the silenced audience allowed him the privilege of hearing the water lapping and the small whispers of a ship at anchor. Then out of the night swooped a Chinese junk, dropping its sails like a huge moth come to rest.

'How beautiful.'

It was Mrs. Rogers. Her thin arms were bare in a long, printed silk dress. Tonight, instead of the straw basket, she carried a large tapestry bag with a tortoise-shell handle. Her features were shadowed. The moon had not yet risen.

Julian murmured a polite nothing. From within there came loud laughter, descending to scattered talk.

'Muriel?'

Mrs. Rogers barely touched Julian's arms. 'Please come with me.'

He wondered why she sounded frightened. That had been her husband's voice. He followed as she hurried to the ladder leading to the ship's lower deck. There, Chinese crew members squatted playing *fan-tan*, slapping down the cards with loud Chinese sounds. Mrs. Rogers walked past them to the bow, standing to look shoreward towards the little, leaping flames of village cooking-fires.

'Muriel?'

Mrs. Rogers had opened her tapestry bag and was holding something out.

'Look,' and he caught a note of hysteria. 'I stole it. Now I don't know what to do with it. Can you help?'

She was holding a phallus from the temple. It was perhaps eighteen inches long. Julian stared, astonished.

'Please. I know it was wrong. Someone—some woman might, I mean . . . Whatever made me do it?'

'Why don't you just chuck it overboard?'

He realised she had expected more, knew he was avoiding the drama she desired.

'You think I should? It might be valuable.'

'Nonsense.' Yet he was stirred by the way she held the polished bit of wood in her long fingers.

'Give it to me,' he said tersely.

'Muriel!'

Rogers was coming down the ladder. Mrs. Rogers left Julian. 'Yes, dear, I'm coming. Let's go back, shall we?'

Alone, Julian stood watching the sea. The ship's whistle blasted the night; the engines shuddered. He tapped the phallus on the railing and began to laugh. If Rich should appear at this moment Julian would hit him, with fist or phallus. It did not matter. The ship churned the water, spray touched his face;

they were again underweigh. Rich did not appear. Too bad.

'Julian? Where are you?'

He did not reply. Deirdre did not really want him. It was more than likely guilt that sent her questing. Let her wait.

His fingers traced the carving of the phallus. To people like Fourscu or Rich or Maggie Veitch, it was an object of obscene laughter, suggesting and hinting perversion. He thought of Mrs. Rogers and her confusion. She thought she had deprived some unknown Siamese woman, being herself deprived.

With a wide swing of his arm, he threw the phallus overboard. The wake foamed, slipping back faster and faster. For a time the phallus would float in the privacy of the night. Eventually, it would be washed up, flotsam on some unknown shore. He leaned over the railing, but saw nothing on the water. Perhaps he should have a wreath of flowers to send after it, like a memorial for the souls of those who drown at sea.

The Hanging Man

There was never silence on the hill. There was never silence anywhere in Singapore. Possibly in the grave, but even there, if the Chinese were to be believed, the newly dead kept joyful assignation with their departed ancestors.

Sweating beneath the mosquito net, legs apart, her nightgown rucked up beneath her breasts, baring her stomach and thighs to whatever random flick of passing air might come that way, Deirdre thought about the Chinese funeral she had attended recently. The procession of mourners carried effigies of everything the dead man had wished to find beyond the grave. Cardboard mockups of concubines; a Rolls Royce; two houses in miniature; furniture; baskets of fruit and flowers; ducks, pressed to paper thin proportions; spices.

And then came the musicians, half a dozen lean men riding in an old Ford van; most of them bare-torsoed, cotton trouser legs rolled up. They blew and twanged and brassily clapped; the screech and whistle and drum beat gradually assumed a familiar form, emerging slowly from cacophony to the recognisable phrases of 'Happy Days are Here Again'. It had all been amusing and splendid material on which to dine out. So much better than Christian funerals, where all was crepuscular and doom-laden, with guilt to be paid for.

As she stood there along with Julian and their friends, resolutely white and ineffably certain they were not being condescending, the idea of guilt bore no relation to their presence by the roadside. They were simply there as viewers. Had it been a Malay funeral, there would have been less gawking. Malays were, after all, indigenous and Nature's Gentlemen. The Chinese were as much invaders as the British. So said

Julian, who enjoyed being negative in the face of conservative opinion.

It would be two or more hours—what was the time?—before the school children in the campong below began their ritual screams, chanting each lesson loudly, throwing away new knowledge on a mindless stream of rote. Did any of that learning mean anything to them? Did it stay? To her it sounded like chaos, but then so much that was Chinese did sound like that even though her friends the Murchisons who were knowledgeable about oriental art and religion and *batik*—he worked for the British Council—insisted Chinese culture was stunningly ordered.

Have to get up. Have to start the day. When she first arrived in the Colony it seemed impossible to keep sleep at bay. She dozed over meals, dozed in the car when the syce drove her on shopping sessions. She found it hard to read and intelligent conversation became an effort. Not that there was much intelligent conversation. Drinking took the place of that. Now, a year on from their arrival, she found it to be an acceptable substitute, even a way of life. People drank to be convivial, to forget a creeping homesickness, to approximate the 'good' life, to compete.

She sat up too quickly, an incipient headache flaring. Damn. A chechak, disturbed by her movement, fled up the wall to freeze upside down on the ceiling. Lizards of happiness. The Malays say a house without them means sorrow. Well, we have enough to last a lifetime of happiness. She had held one once, pulsating in the mould of her hand, cold and wholly reptilian; nothing to indicate happiness.

Stretching carefully, she took a deep breath. Her hair was damp with sweat and she loosened it from her neck; a warm shower, to be followed by a delicious sponge bath from the Ali Baba jar. She hoped Ah Kwong had remembered to fill it. She lifted the mosquito net and sat for a moment on the edge of the bed, one of twins she and Julian had moved together to give more scope for their lovemaking. Julian got up at 6.00 a.m. All the European men in Singapore got up at 6.00 to work while it was still relatively cool. The children arose at that hour as well. Her five-year-old son was with his *amah* now, pushed along in his wheeled chair, or trotting on the safety of grassy verges where the Chinese liked to give their caged birds an airing.

Deirdre glanced briefly at Julian's side of the beds. In the best romantic tradition she should be thinking tenderly of last night. It wasn't all that romantic, though it should have been. Several people had told her she and Julian were considered the most decorative young couple in the Colony, an opinion borne out by frequent invitations to Government House. Not for the general garden party to which most people were invited, but to small, intimate dinners, featuring up-country sultans.

'So picturesque in their beautiful sarongs.'

The remark had been made by an American woman from the meagre US section of the island, the wife of a business representative, or some such thing. The Americans were not always acceptable, except in matters of commerce. Julian enjoyed quoting this particular woman's hyperbole, but nevertheless himself bought and wore a plum-coloured sarong fraught with gold threads. Only at home in the evenings, of course. 'The coolest possible garment' he liked to tell random visitors passing through Singapore. In fact, his strong legs showed to advantage.

The houseboy Ah Kwong coughed outside one of the half-doors opening from bedroom to verandah.

'Mem?'

'Thank you, *t'rimah kasi*. I'm coming.'

He wanted her to know the bath was ready. Ah Kwong wasted no words. He went about his duties silently and efficiently. It was only lately a tension had developed between them. Deirdre found this disturbing.

She thought about it as she sluiced cool water from the Ali Baba jar over her slender body. The tiled floor was clammy and a cockroach two inches long waved its feelers at her as she bent to soap her legs. She shuddered. Loathsome things. Yet

Ah Kwong, sweeping them off the walls and cracking their spines, gave them to Cookie to fry in oil. A Chinese delicacy. She closed the thought away, concentrating on what she must do to make her peace with the houseboy. He was such a marvellous servant. Everyone said so. Trustworthy. And beautiful, Deirdre added privately. It was not an adjective to be applied publicly to a Chinese houseboy. Ah Kwong had soft eyes and the most delicate of eyebrows. His white uniform was impeccable, rigid with starch. Nowadays his ubiquitous smile, termed by Julian who enjoyed the obvious cliché, inscrutable, began to irritate.

He really is inscrutable, thought Deirdre, trying to dry herself on a towel smelling of mildew. But her pores oozed sweat and she knew powder would gather lumpily in the creases of her body if she used the puff. What was the use?

Dressed and seated under the whirling teak fan above the dining-room table, she felt better and ate fresh mangosteen and toast with appetite. Her hangover seemed better. She was on her second cup of coffee when Julian arrived for breakfast. He bent to kiss her, smelling of starch and sweat. He wore the regulation garment of well-placed Singapore colonials: a collarless white jacket buttoned to the throat with matching white trousers. He looked hot, his black hair combed smoothly back. The *Tuan Besar*. The boss. A bank manager at twenty-nine with a big future ahead. Apparently solid and dependable, he had a capricious streak which Deirdre feared, knowing him capable of reversing an opinion in the midst of argument just for the sake of being perverse. Bloody-minded, she called it. Julian laughed at being an Empire Builder but enjoyed the idea of a possible knighthood, even while he mocked it. His general attitude made for insecurity and Deirdre was already insecure in this country of contrasts with its extraordinary beauty, discomfort, and where there was no twilight.

'Any plans for today?' Julian was looking at her over the top of his newspaper.

She pulled her thoughts back. 'Yes. I'll take Billy to the

Swimming Club this morning and I'll read to him after his nap. After that I have to play Mah-Jong. Don't forget the party at the Dutch Consulate tonight.'

She felt cheerful. Things to do. The little Chinese shoemaker in Middle Road should have her gold slippers finished by now; she would need them for the dance at Tanglin Club on Saturday night. And there was her new dress to be picked up.

The Chinese school children were in full tongue by now. Their babble rose above the perpetual insect song. Ah Kwong, bringing more coffee, displaced the heavy air briefly so that she caught the thick scent of frangipani blossoms. A huge bowl of them sat on the verandah coffee table.

The singsong of Loo Ah Loke's voice was heard down the drive. A moment later Billy charged across the polished tiles, pushing rugs out of place as he ran. Ah Kwong frowned, settling the rugs back in place with his toes.

'Darling!'

Deirdre kissed her son's silky hair. He wore a diminutive sunsuit and his back was slippery with sweat.

'Big ships! Big, big ships!'

'Yes, baby. Big ships.'

Loo Ah Loke regarded them benevolently. She carried Billy's cardigan, convinced there was danger in even the lightest breeze. Her eyes were gentle, the weight of her black hair pulled back into a big knot. She washed it once a month and when loosened it fell below her knees. One of the band of *amahs* in the province from China, a quiet matriarchy, save when they encountered one another in an explosion of cackles and screechings, Loo Ah Loke had come to earn money to keep her two children left behind in China. It was their way, Ah Kwong explained to Deirdre. These women did not marry. He seemed to find this amusing, and there was always something derisive in his tone when he spoke in Cantonese with the *amah*.

The telephone rang. Another invitation to a party. It rang again. There would be a tennis foursome tomorrow.

'You're getting too thin,' remarked Julian. 'It's all this exercise.'

'No, I'm melting away in the heat. I wish we had air-conditioning.'

'Hah! Not even the Governor has air-conditioning. You know that,' Julian rose to go. 'It's time we had another cocktail party. Can you make out a list?'

He took his briefcase from Ah Kwong and a moment later Deirdre heard his car drive away.

Ah Kwong was by her side. A gold tooth accentuated his grin. 'Mem, Said ask when you want car.'

There was no real humour in his smile. Nor was he obsequious. She felt again the tension. It had something to do with the porcelain teaset he had dropped. Guilt perhaps. She had been annoyed at the time, wondering if his salary should be docked, although he did not earn that much. When she told Julian he asked if the teaset was Japanese.

'What's that got to do with it?'

'Everything. There's a war going on between China and Japan, you know. A lot of people are being killed.'

But it was all so remote. China and Japan. She could not absorb the fact of war, or connect it in anyway with the broken teaset. Yet she supposed there were Chinese trapped on the island or up country, unable to return to their own land and their families because of the war. These, of course, were not Straits-born Chinese, only itinerant workers. Invaders, as Julian had said.

Deirdre ordered the car to take her and Billy to the Swimming Club. Loo Ah Loke too, of course. The *amah* sat in front beside Said who looked very small behind the Ford's steering wheel.

On the way home—she had lunched at the Swimming Club to give Billy a treat—Deirdre stopped to buy a new teaset. It was slightly different from the first, but with equally lovely colours. Ah Kwong had better take care. It was rather expensive.

He was waiting at the bottom of the steps as the car drove

up. So was the syce's small boy, with whom Billy played. Now he ran off with 'Syce-boy'—Deirdre had not thought to learn his real name—and Ah Kwong carried Deirdre's packages into the house. She sank on to the pretty chintz couch. Massed flowers in jars were set about the room. Arranging them was one of her great pleasures. One could be extravagant, there were so many, and orchids were almost boring. She breathed in their fragrance, delighting in it after the stench of the Singapore River through which they had just driven. The fan hummed and except for the ever-present insect voices and the distant susurration of city sounds, the room approximated peace.

Deirdre closed her eyes. In a minute she would call for a cold drink. She wondered if she should serve *satay* at the cocktail party, meat skewered and cooked by the roadside in Hokien Street. A few people liked it, but a lot thought it was dangerous. Worms, you know, they said.

A crash came from the depths of the house. She stiffened, guessing the sound's origin. He's done it again. But she did not move. She seldom made an unnecessary movement because of the heat.

Ah Kwong did not appear. She called 'Boy-ee-ee!'

When they first arrived in Singapore, Deirdre and Julian had considered this form of address far too patronising. But gradually, as the heat eroded their determination not to behave like cliché colonials, they found it easier to shout the diminutive. Chinese names did not lend themselves easily to the tongue. When summoned, Ah Kwong became 'boy'.

'Mem?' The usual grin.

'Did you drop something just now?'

He continued to smile. 'Yahyah. Box no good.'

'The box? You mean you dropped the teaset?'

'Yah.'

She meant to be angry. But it took too much effort.

'You are careless, Ah Kwong. Did it break?' As if she didn't know.

'Yah, yah.'

She could think of nothing to say. Of course, he had done it on purpose.

Ah Kwong was watching her. 'Mem not buy Japanese sings. *Tidah bagus*. No good.'

'It was a beautiful set.'

'No good,' he repeated stubbornly, and stood waiting.

She sighed. 'Bring me a lemon squash, Ah Kwong.'

He left. She visualised a silent vendetta, she buying the teasets, he breaking them, set after set. She felt irritated, put upon. All because of some stupid war somewhere. But that was not the way to think.

She supposed she should feel guilty. But all she could bring her mind to focus on was the list of guests she must make for the imminent cocktail party. As she sat writing at a teakwood desk at the far end of the verandah, there came a swelling, sonorous sound. She ran to the wide window, unshuttered and unscreened, though bats and insects flew in and out when the lights were on. There below the hill where they lived, its masts mingling with the big trees lining the Straits channel, she saw a liner flying the American flag.

Oh, marvellous! Tomorrow there would be frozen lettuce in the Cold Storage shop. Well in time for the party.

The next week Julian slept late the morning after their gathering which by Singapore standards had been extremely successful and engendered reciprocal invitations, necessary for Julian's advancement. Around about 10.00 p.m. everyone was drunk enough to think of going dancing, which they did, at 'Eddie's' a night club on the sea front. Then on to someone's house and midnight swimming with no 'God Save the King' to interrupt.

Deirdre slowly surfaced from sleep to hear Billy chattering with his father in the bathroom. She lay quietly for a moment, wondering if vertigo would attack once she sat up. Not so bad. Billy ran into the room. He looked frantic.

'Mummy! Mummy! There's a man, a man in the tree!'

Julian appeared behind his son. 'This is one of his wildest

tales yet. Take him, will you? I want to shave.'

Deirdre helped Billy through the mosquito net, cuddling him close. He pushed his head against her shoulder. She felt the rapid beat of his heart, and was afraid.

'Baby, baby, what is it!'

'Where's *amah*?' asked Julian. 'Damn woman, she ought to be looking after him.' Julian had a hangover.

'Man,' murmured Billy, still tight against her. There were tears on his round, pale cheeks. 'Man in the tree . . .'

'Where, darling? What man? Where is the tree?'

For an answer, Billy scrambled off the bed, tangling himself in the mosquito net. Julian freed him, and the child ran from them, but a moment later returned.

'Mummy?'

Deirdre looked at her husband who said nothing.

'I'm going to find out what he's talking about,' she said.

'It's just one of his crazy notions. We'll have to take him to the doctor.'

'I don't think he's making it up.'

Deirdre pulled on a housecoat and followed Billy down the steps. In the driveway he took her hand and held it tightly. Julian, looking irritated, followed them down a side path that led to the tennis court. As they reached the court, they stopped dead. A small group of people stood by the fence. There was Said, Ah Kwong, Loo Ah Loke, their Tamil gardener, a burly Sikh whom she recognised as a night watchman from a government building down the road. There were also two strange Chinese. All of them were staring up at the big flame-of-the-forest tree which stood just outside the tennis-court fence.

'Oh God! There is a man.'

And there was. She saw his bare feet below dark work trousers—Chinese coolie dress, except for the felt hat on the brim of which a scarlet flame-of-the-forest petal had settled. The group below the tree was silent.

Deirdre could not move. The body hung there, the head

tilted. From where she stood, the dead man's face could not be seen.

'Mem?' It was Ah Kwong. He did not touch her. 'You come with Billy.'

How could he smile that way! But she went with him, up the driveway back to the house. The *amah* came behind. She was uttering clicking noises and muttering. Behind her walked Said, looking frightened.

'*Itu hantu*,' he said.

'What does he mean?' Deirdre realised she sounded querulous. But I'm afraid. No, I'm not, except for Billy. Could he have seen the man's face?

'Ali says it is a ghost. But not. Man kill himself.'

'But why?'

'Maybe he family killed by Japanese.'

Killed by the Japanese. Flatly, like that. She sat on the couch, holding Billy, who suddenly struggled free, calling for Syceboy. Deirdre let him go. *Amah* was there. She waited, trying to imagine what the hanging man's face would look like, then shrinking away from the thought.

She called Ah Kwong. He brought her a brandy which she drank quickly. Julian returned looking pale.

'I'll have to call the police.'

Later, when it was all over, they took up the pattern of their usual Saturday. Lunch with the Murchisons, discussing the suicide. Julian had recovered but was drinking rather too much. He had no idea, he said, how long the man had been hanging there. No one was talking, and they certainly would not have cut down the poor devil. The Malays were too superstitious; the Indians washed their hands of it; the Chinese, had they cut him down, would, by their ethics, have had to care for and feed the dead man's relatives for the rest of their lives. A bad bargain.

Deirdre did not say much. It had become another dining-out story, except that a man had died. She wondered how great a shock Billy had received. He seemed all right. Children recovered quickly, Julian told her, apparently forgetting his own fears that Billy should be over-stimulated.

She watched her husband, tall, affable, talking busily, a glass in his hand, enjoying the occasion. Perhaps she was being unfair. *It was Julian who first told me about the war.*

The matter was dropped. No police came to ask questions. The body had been removed and no doubt swiftly disposed of because of the heat. No happy funeral procession for this lonely *hantu*. Perhaps what he had wanted he could not have taken with him, having already lost it.

Time began again. They went to parties and gave parties. Julian worked and Deirdre played tennis. They both danced and drank. Deirdre watched for signs of lasting shock in Billy. There seemed none. He continued his fantasies, but he had no nightmares. She relaxed.

One afternoon, a month later, Deirdre came home from a tennis match to find the house empty. Ah Kwong did not meet her. Perhaps it was one of his days off, which he took at random, usually leaving a young assistant, the *kitchi*, or little one, in charge. Or possibly he had gone on an errand. She sat thinking about Ah Kwong. Since the hanging they had been more friendly. She guessed he was aware now that she understood his need to break the teaset. She thought of Billy, whom she must fetch soon from a children's party. He would be overtired and overfed, but the party would help him forget past events. At least she hoped so.

Getting up she wandered into her son's room. It was as always immaculate. Billy's mosquito net had been draped back from his cot which was made up with sheets printed with nursery scenes. Loo Ah Loke's sleeping mat was rolled up at the end of her narrow bed. Toys were . . .

Deirdre gasped. Her eyes now accepted what she had not at first noticed. Hanging from the cot, their necks encircled tightly by string, were all of Billy's toys: stuffed animals, a boat, Punch and Judy, and most distressing of all, his favourite bear, Sinbad, a lifeless row, an extension of Billy's fears, terrifying in their significance.

Deirdre stood as unmoving as though there before her she saw again the hanging man with his bare feet and the scarlet flame-of-the-forest petal on his hat. She felt tears on her face. Behind her there was a small sound and she turned to see Ah Kwong. He stared at the slaughtered row on the cot and for a moment his smile faded. He murmured something in Cantonese.

'Ah Kwong...'

But already he had gone. She looked again at the cot, sweeping the back of one hand across her cheeks to remove her tears. Billy—a baby exposed to war; it had come into this room.

Ah Kwong returned. He held a pair of scissors and began to cut down the toys.

'No, I'll do it.'

She took the shears, snipped and snipped, handing the toys to him until she came to Sinbad. String was embedded so deeply into his swivelled neck that she could not loosen it.

Ah Kwong stood silently watching; he did not attempt to help. She pulled and twisted, but the string remained stubbornly tight. She began to sob.

'I'm sorry, I'm sorry,' but to whom she was apologising she was not sure.

The string attaching Sinbad to the cot snapped suddenly and the bear dropped into her hand, his black button eyes staring blindly, his half-severed head dropping sideways.

Beside her, Ah Kwong still said nothing.

Here Comes Our Sunset

Deirdre was never quite certain when her uneasiness had begun. Perhaps it had always been there, activated from time to time by small, isolated moments of fear, like the evening when, alone in the bungalow, she had watched the greatly enlarged shadows of a chechak fighting a praying mantis in a dance of death. The lizard won, darting behind a picture with the crushed insect in its mouth. Even now, Deirdre did not like to remember that eerie drama.

Perhaps this vague anxiety was just due to missing Billy. She had not really wanted him to go to school, but had yielded because Julian convinced her the cooler temperatures of the hills would be good for the child. Singapore's unrelenting heat and humidity took their toll, even of a healthy child. They had come out from England in 1937, over a year ago, and Deirdre still felt she would never be really cool again. Now, listening to the whirr and whisper of the big teak ceiling-fan in her living room, she was aware again of a half-buried fear and an emptiness that spread out and away from her, taking no account of the seething, noisy life in the streets and on the quays below the hill where they lived.

'I feel so alien,' she had said to Julian, trying to explain to him as well as to herself the state of her emotions. 'I feel superimposed.'

He had smiled in the superior way he usually reserved for those he considered, in his words, 'Scots and English coolies'.

'We're all superimposed,' he replied. 'But not for long.'

'What do you mean?'

'Nothing,' he said, 'nothing at all.'

And she could get no further with him. Why must he be so

26

cryptic? Lately, he was more than that. He was positively strange. And he drank too much. At twenty-nine, Julian's good looks were alloyed by the kind of quiet cynicism that made heartier people draw away from him after a time. Gregarious herself, Deirdre felt impelled to defend her husband until she realised it made no difference to him one way or another.

She sighed. It couldn't still be that one time when she had almost been unfaithful to him. It was over now; they had discussed it, putting the episode down to the absurd ratio of the sexes: at least thirty men to one woman. Too easy, really. Conscious of her attraction, Deirdre sometimes found her popularity a burden. Constant flattery was eroding. She had come to accept it, however, and in so doing had acquired a certain coarsening of personality. Other women in their jealousy saw this as deliberate self-approval; men talked of her among themselves, but never crudely. They were too romantic in their desire. Besides, she was married. They envied Julian, an envy based on dislike. Julian was not one of the boys. He hated cricket and held unacceptable theories about creed and colour. Once he had put up for membership at the exclusive Tanglin Club a Jewish friend of his, a rubber planter. It had all been fearfully embarrassing, because, of course, the petition had been turned down. The recent arrival on the island of Jewish refugees from Hitler's Germany, a tiny quota, bore no relationship in most people's minds to the incident of the rubber planter. Indeed, when Julian started taking flute lessons from a sad-eyed Berlin musician, Herr Fenichel, everyone congratulated him on his humanity. For a short time, he became 'good old Julian', their eccentric friend who played the flute.

Deirdre, a mildly good pianist, sometimes accompanied Julian. It was a dubious duet, Herr Fenichel the moderator. Since he knew practically no English, progress was slow. But Deirdre became fond of Herr Fenichel, who, as well as sad eyes, had a long tapir-nose. She knew that in the evenings he played with a dance band in a club by the sea. She had seen him there and had waved from the dancefloor. What did he make of the

'Lambeth Walk', she wondered. She also wondered where he slept. Where did anyone sleep who wasn't British or rich Chinese? The Sikh watchmen, the *jagars*, slept on pallets outside the buildings they guarded. *Amahs* slept on thin mattresses, rolled up during the day. The Malays slept under *atap* roofs. But where did poor Herr Fenichel sleep? She grieved for him in his heavy, European-style suit. What a monster Hitler was. Yet it was all very far away.

She heard a car drive up. Julian, at last. He had been coming home later and later. They hadn't made love for weeks. There was something secretive about him these days, something she did not understand. Yet, instinctively, she knew it was not another woman. She knew, even though the possibility was there. Instead of walking to work and back, he had begun to use the Rover, leaving Deirdre with their Ford de luxe which the syce Said always drove. What did Julian do during these absent hours? When she asked, he said non-committally, 'Extra work'.

Today she had something important to tell him. They had been invited by the GOC's aide-de-camp to hear the big 15-inch guns fired, those guns that were Singapore's defence against invasion, the guns that made them all, even Herr Fenichel, sleep safely. It was a gala occasion, with drinks and dressing-up. Fun.

Julian, looking hot, bent to kiss her. She smelled beer. When she told him about the guns he said, 'Good God!' and walked into the bedroom. She felt let down, then, as she always did in the face of Julian's lack of enthusiasm, began to wonder if perhaps the whole affair were not, after all, rather unnecessary. A bit comic-opera; Gilbert and Sullivan.

Julian returned wearing shorts and a thin, open-necked shirt. He had washed and sleeked down his dark hair.

'So we'll be there with all the *Tuan-tuan Besar*,' he said. 'A gathering of self-congratulation.'

He was in one of his moods. She felt irritated.

'They must know what they're doing,' she said. 'I don't think you should gibe.'

'My dear girl. With Japanese troops thirty miles from Hong Kong, how can I be gibing?'

'But we're not at war with the Japanese.'

'We will be.'

She felt the familiar, lost floundering that Julian's apparently indisputable statements always aroused in her. How did he know?

'How do you know?' she asked, and took a long drink from the *pahit*, consisting of gin, lime and ice that Ah Kwong had just set before her.

'It's obvious to anyone who thinks. The Nips want Malaya.'

'The Nips!' Not one of Julian's words. He *was* in a mood.

'They have everything sewed up,' Julian went on. 'Infiltration is the name of the game. I'll bet you Echigoya is the spy headquarters.'

'Echigoya!' It was a Japanese textile shop, selling beautiful cottons and silks. She often went there. It was as familiar a port of call as Robinson's for coffee. 'I hope you're wrong.'

'Don't think about it now. Victor wants us to meet him for a drink at the Sea View.'

Victor was their Jewish friend, the rubber planter. A short ticker tape of doubt ran through her mind and was dismissed. The Sea View was one of the safe places. Victor would not be turned away.

'I think his new girlfriend will be with him,' Julian said.

'The gorgeous Eurasian?'

'The same.'

'Was the flag out?'

'Yes.'

They looked at each other and broke into laughter. Victor lived near the beach in comfortable solitude. Being rich, he catered elegantly for his needs: lavish food parcels sent from Fortnum and Mason; the best wines; the most beautiful women. Whenever he had one of these latter in residence, or in bed, he hung out a white flag, indicating his need for privacy. His friends respected this wish.

'He was in the bank earlier looking pleased with himself. When I drove home, the flag was out.'

'Victor and his women...' She pretended amused disdain. Actually, she was pleased to see that Julian's dark mood was lifting. She too felt better. As long as there were things to do, her malaise did not manifest itself. The Eurasian girl would certainly be attractive. Victor's girls always had something special about them. Her thoughts turned to what she would wear—not that there was any question of competing. The girl, after all, was Eurasian. Her scope was limited. Deirdre did not articulate these thoughts. In fact, she scarcely realised she had them. Having a Eurasian as a friend in Singapore was tantamount to riding a bicycle, which only natives did. Deirdre, purchasing and riding a bicycle herself, was regarded as being as amusingly eccentric as her husband. But the Colony forgave her because she was close enough to the Governor to exercise his wife's hunter. It gave Deirdre a kick to tell people at dinner parties that she got to Government House through the stables.

Although she enjoyed riding and sat a horse well, Deirdre maintained certain qualms which she managed to conceal. The horse, a big Australian gelding, behaved itself most of the time, but the jungle trails where she rode seemed unfriendly. She strove visually to change the landscape, to reduce it to the green hedgerows of nostalgia. But the huge trees, the creepers, the wait-a-bit thorns, the sudden slashing blue flight of a kingfisher, remained intractably foreign. She recognised the beauty, but could not contain it. The last time she had gone riding, she had lost her way. The brief twilight soon slipped into darkness and she had been forced to give the horse its head, cowering in the saddle as the night voices of the jungle began. Reason told her the island was too small to be totally lost and presently the horse found its way out. But the experience had augmented Deirdre's general fear. She said nothing to Julian but ever since—though it had not been long ago—found excuses not to ride.

On the day the guns were to be fired, she dressed carefully. Clothes were part of the fun. She tried not to wear the same dress too often, and consequently her big teak cupboard was crammed. Sometimes mildew forced her to throw out nearly new garments. Today, she wore a dress by Lanvin, sent to her by a friend in Paris. It was blue and grey striped organdie with puffed sleeves, and with it she wore a little veiled hat cocked over one eye. It was an occasion for hats, like the races.

Close to the waterfront, the huge guns gleamed ominously. Guests were placed in rattan chairs at strategic angles so that repercussion from the firing would not offend sensitive eardrums. Drinks in sweating glasses were passed by white-jacketed messboys. Sailors were busy with ammunition; flags fluttered; the women's clothes made bright patches; and on the quiet sea a Navy launch waited to pull its floating target within range. The entire scene suggested a painting by Raoul Dufy.

Although it was the Navy's day, a few Air Force officers were present. Deirdre recognised Neal MacInnis, a curly-headed Scots lieutenant, and waved to him. Immediately he came to stand by her chair, watching with her as the floating target came into view.

A gun was fired. Water sprayed high. Another shot, this time a hit, and the watchers patted their hands together and cried 'Bravo!' More drinks were served.

Neal did not clap or exclaim. She was aware of his proximity, feeling excited. Turning her head, she saw Julian standing a few yards away talking with Mr. Foster, a high-ranking civil servant. But his eyes were on her, and she guessed what he was thinking. But if I'm randy, she thought, it's your fault. And don't think I didn't notice how you flirted with Victor's Eurasian girl. Still, she had been beautiful.

Another blast from the guns, sending shivers of sound through the hot afternoon.

'Oh, splendid!'

'Good show!'

'Marvellous!'

Around her the satisfaction and sense of achievement thickened. It was fine; it was grand; it was what they had expected.

'Those guns will be useless if an attack comes in Johore.' Neal MacInnis bent over her, speaking quietly. 'The Air Force will be the first line of defence.'

He was overheard. 'Shame,' said a woman Deirdre had seen but did not know. A Navy wife, she thought. 'You are out of line.'

Neal flushed to the roots of his close-cut red curls. Deirdre wanted to comfort him. He was said to be homesick and frequently played his bagpipes along the cliffs near his barracks. Deirdre had heard them. Oddly, the sound blended with the tropical night. When she mentioned this later to Julian he said it was to be expected.

'The Scots have no priority on pipes. In fact, they came originally from India.'

He said this with a throwaway tone, indicating the facts were there for anyone to find if enough patience were involved, which he had, willy-nilly.

Deirdre preferred to associate bagpipes with Scotland. Neal MacInnis and his homesickness touched her. When the last gun had been fired—'Ah, bad luck, a miss'—she invited him for a drink, an invitation he eagerly accepted.

Following the firing of the guns, life returned to normal. Yet a fever invested the island. There were more and more parties, heavier drinking, wreckless behaviour. Abruptly, the far-off phoney war ended and a real one began. Its declaration acted briefly, like a deep breath, held collectively, then exhaled on a huge sigh, almost of relief. Hitler would have his comeuppance now.

Julian and Deirdre drove up to Fraser's Hill to collect Billy. The little boy's presence helped Deirdre to forget a growing interest in Neal MacInnis. Besides, Billy, and Billy's needs, allayed her continued anxieties.

The months passed. 1940 was celebrated by a fancy-dress ball at the Tanglin Club. Three people fell into the swimming pool. Signs of war appeared in the arrival of British submarines. Julian and Deirdre met some of the young officers, and Deirdre took Billy with her to visit the convoluted bowels of a submarine skippered by a young officer who declared his love. It was all part of the fever.

Neal MacInnis, infatuated, asked her to go for a walk one day. They wandered into a Chinese graveyard below the bungalow where tombstones canted unevenly. There came a wild scatter of explosions and Neal went white, gasped and began to shake.

'Yes, I know,' he said when Deirdre pointed out the sound was only Chinese firecrackers. 'It's nerves. I'm a bloody coward, you know.'

Rumours of German pocket battleships, the *Gneisenau* and the *Scharnhorst* were rife. They had been seen; they had not been seen. People went on drinking. Social intercourse was like a long, ever wilder New Year's Eve party. Herr Fenichel continued to give Julian lessons though communication was still limited. Only when he illustrated a passage of Bach on the flute did a light, quickly dimmed, appear in his eyes.

Deirdre, restless, formed the habit of walking along the docks by the godowns, taking Billy with her. They would sit, huddled together on a ship's bollard, watching the busy coolies and Tamil dock workers. Then this innocent occupation came to an end when the military banned free coming and going of traffic to Collyer Quay.

Early in the spring—though the seasons all ran into each other without apparent change—an invitation to dinner came from the Fosters. Deirdre dreaded it. The Fosters were so much older; they were patronising. She hoped Julian would behave. She hoped there would be other guests. But it turned out to be just the four of them.

'We thought a quiet evening,' said Mrs. Foster, spreading and maternal in flowered silk. 'Because of . . . things. You know.'

During dinner, no one mentioned the war. Julian asked his host about early days in the Colony. Deirdre and Mrs. Foster spoke of servants. Mrs. Foster said they were not as they used to be. There was a radical element among them. Still, things changed. One supposed they had to, somehow. The world... She did not finish, her still youthful eyes looking bewildered.

After dinner, Mr. Foster suggested coffee and brandy in the garden. They settled in deck chairs and a houseboy wrapped canvas around their legs to guard against mosquitoes. Fans, imprinted with advertisements for Tiger Beer, were distributed. Deirdre fanned limply, hearing the zing of mosquitoes. She looked at her legs in their wrapping and was reminded suddenly of the voyage out when the barber aboard their P & O liner had died of heat in the Red Sea. He had been buried instantly, his body sliding from under the Union Jack into the sea's depths with a faint splash. Deirdre could not understand why the flag had been kept, jerked away at the last moment.

'They'll need it for the next one,' said Julian when she asked him. 'Have you seen the crew's quarters?'

It had not been a satisfactory answer. How could she have seen the crew's quarters?

'Won't be long now,' said Mr. Foster.

He let out a triumphant shout, startling everyone. 'Look, look! Here comes our sunset! Never tire of it. In all my years out here, never miss it. Always the same. Beautiful!'

And it was. The colours spilled into each other with a splendid carelessness. They blended and gradually faded away, leaving only a long stripe of transluscent green, paler than emeralds, tinged with gold.

'Finished,' said Mr. Foster. 'Now we can go inside.'

They ended the evening at a nightclub, but not the one where Mr. Fenichel played. Deirdre was glad of this. His mournful face disturbed her dance steps. By the time they arrived home, she was rather drunk and knew that Julian must be more so, though he showed it less. He ran up the steps ahead of her as she lingered to say goodnight to Said. When the car had driven off, she still did not go indoors, listening to the pleading wails of a Malay song from some hidden radio in the kampong below.

It ceased and she mounted the steps, brushing at moths as they danced their ballet around the porch light. Twice she had seen a lunar moth, large as a baby's head, exquisite in design but terrifying in its stealthy texture, brushing her face without warning. Remembering it made her remember also the *kengwah* plant in its pot by the front door. The *kengwah* only bloomed occasionally, opening its great single white flower in a burst of overwhelming fragrance before it died. If one were quick enough, the moment of blooming could be watched, the huge, tumescent bud, suddenly alive, pealing back, unfurling its beauty minute by minute. Deirdre and Julian had seen this happen once in their three and a half years. They always meant to watch for the blooming, but somehow forgot, coming too late, finding the flower already wilting.

But tonight Deirdre saw the *kengwah* was almost ready. She ran in to tell Julian, determined that this time she would not miss its glory. Julian was not in the living room. She went quietly into Billy's room, reassured by his soft breathing. The *amah* slept on her pallet at the foot of Billy's bed.

Julian was in the spare room. He had changed into his sarong and baju, a conceit he carried off well, not only because the Malay clothing suited him but because he assured everyone of its coolness. Only common sense, he said.

He stood now in the front of the *almirah*—a black teakwood cupboard. Tonight it looked less like an upright coffin because its doors were open. Deirdre stared. It occurred to her that she had not been in this room for weeks, but obviously Julian had. The cupboard was stacked with tinned goods, dozens of brightly coloured cans, beans, stew, butter, soup, puddings, tinned milk, piled neatly, filling the large cupboard halfway to its ceiling.

'Julian! What is it? What have you done?'

He turned, a familiar Cross & Blackwell tin in his hands.

'Supplies. There'll be a siege, you know. Must be prepared.'

'A siege!'

'Yes. The Japanese will want this island.'

'But the Navy—the guns.'

He sounded so certain; yet wasn't he just a trifle silly, standing there in his sarong which sagged a little below the beer belly he had recently acquired? He had turned away, and was examining and fingering his stores possessively.

She thought of everything she had heard people say; of the emphasis laid on Singapore's impregnability. He was drunk at this moment, but he could not have been drunk all these weeks when he was laying in his supplies. She remembered Neal's reaction to the Chinese fireworks. They were all suffering from war nerves. But it was all so far away...

Julian was holding a large tin of Carnation evaporated milk. His eyes were very dark, almost black. She sensed something new. Fear. Not Julian. Julian could not be afraid. Yet he had once told her that to acknowledge fear was itself a form of bravery.

'Julian, I don't understand.'

'You've got to.' He shook the tin angrily. 'You must think of Billy. Day after tomorrow you and he leave for Australia. I've already booked your passage.'

'Australia!'

'Yes. I'll follow when I can.'

Feeling panic, Deirdre stood there in silence. They stared at one another, not hearing the metallic resonance of a million insect voices.

'Loo Ah Loke can go with you.'

Mention of the *amah* brought a return to reality. She heard again the night sounds, became aware of Chinese music in the distance.

'It's all so sudden.'

'Not for me. I've been thinking and planning for months.'

'You should have told me.'

'You wouldn't have agreed.'

'What makes you think I'll agree now?'

'Your own intelligence and concern for Billy.'

He was right, but she still held back, forced into rage by the knowledge that he was so often right.

'Aren't you assuming rather a lot?'

'Damn it, there isn't time to argue. You've got a lot of packing to do.'

Again he shook the tin of milk which abruptly exploded, covering Julian's face and head with sticky liquid. A stream of white ran down onto his purple baju, making a mockery of heroics. She giggled nervously, but felt only love.

'Oh, Julian, darling...'

'Get me a towel,' he said coldly, and set down the tin. 'Bloody thing. Probably the heat. Or a fault in the metal.'

She went for a towel. What if they all exploded, showering the room in myriad colours, themselves a travesty of sunset.

'I'll need a drink after this,' he said, wiping away the mess. 'Call Ah Kwong.'

'He'll be asleep.'

'Wake him. I want a double gin *pahit*.'

She did as she was told, hoping Ah Kwong would forgive them. Julian was usually thoughtful of the servants' welfare if only, she sometimes thought, not to emulate his fellow colonials.

Having delivered the order to a sleepy houseboy, shouting through the back door leading to the servants' quarters, knowing she would be waking a number of people, Deirdre walked back through the living room, remembering then the *kengwah* bud.

Bending over the pot, she saw excitedly that it was beginning to open. Already a perfume stole from the as yet unfolded petals. She thought of calling Julian but remembered something had changed between them. He was asking her to go away. Untrue. He was sending her away for her own good. And Billy's good. She heard a thump and rattle from the spare room, nodded at Ah Kwong as he walked past on bare feet carrying Julian's drink on a tray. She looked again at the *kengwah*. It was wider now.

'Ah Kwong!' she called. Ah Kwong, not Julian.

'Mem?'

He was there beside her, smiling, imperturbable. She pointed.

'Look, it's blooming.'

He nodded vigorously. 'Yah. *Itu banyak bagus*. It is very good.'

Then he was gone, sensibly, back to his bed, his pallet. She continued to stare at the great flower as it opened, petal by creamy petal, while its fragrance seemed to fill the night. The sweetness was unbearable. She felt tears in her eyes.

'So it's bloomed.'

Julian stood there, drink in hand. A dollop of evaporated milk still clung to his black hair. She began to cry. The *kengwah* fragrance proliferated, binding them together in a sensuous cloud. But by morning the blossom would be dead, would be gone like everything else here she had known for so brief a time, had known, repudiated and loved.

'Don't cry, darling,' Julian said. 'There's no time for crying.'

This is my Mistress

On my way home to the United States from Malaya in 1940, I found myself with a fortnight's wait between ships in Hong Kong. The city was ominous with troops, and a melancholy surge of refugees from the mainland filled the streets. Wondering what to do with myself, I remembered that Desmond James must still be teaching in Hong Kong and I telephoned at once to make an appointment, hoping that his cordiality would extend itself as far as a friend of a friend, which was all I was.

It did. The next afternoon I was summoned back to my hotel from the beach, where a quiet sea mocked the frightening proximity of barbed wire and the horizon appeared limitless to my lonely gaze. Desmond was waiting for me in the lobby, his short, plump figure hovering diffidently close to the door, and when he saw me approaching, he hurried across the verandah.

'This is splendid,' he said in a light, rather breathless voice and I noticed with astonishment that he was blushing. His eyes behind their round spectacles were gleaming with a friendliness which was irresistible and I realised suddenly how shy he must be. He wore, as evident sop to the Empire and his profession, a tweed suit, but the immense foulard cravat, flaring out from beneath his double chin, gave him the air of an 18th-century cherub.

'My dear,' he said, piloting me a little fussily towards the driveway, 'you must take all your meals with me. How awful for you, staying in that hotel. The food . . .'

His voice died on the word with such a tone of disgust that immediately I understood the hotel meals which I had accepted uncritically must, in reality, be of the lowest standard.

Drooping over the wheel of Desmond's car, an open roadster

39

of uncertain age, was an exquisitely handsome Chinese boy
with gentle eyes and brows like two brush strokes.

'Chung, my cook and chauffeur,' said Desmond. He helped
me into the back seat. 'I have never felt that I could reach the
state of intimacy with motorcars which is required to drive
them. In fact, I think it would be reprehensible of me to try.'
We set off through the hills and as I held my hat and fought
for breath I wondered if, although a creation of beauty, Chung
too should not be considered reprehensible as a chauffeur.

The car finally stopped because the road itself ended at the
foot of a steep hill covered with what seemed to me to be
impenetrable brush. But even as I looked, a man emerged from
a thicket with two pails on a stick slung across his back.

'My waterboy,' said Desmond. 'Everything has to be taken
up on foot.' He offered this information with such an air of
satisfaction that I felt the virtue of foot-travel could not be
questioned.

We began to climb through the heavy undergrowth, following a well-worn path that rose steeply ahead, Desmond in
the lead.

In about twenty minutes we had reached the top, emerging
at the side of a clearing where a low, rose-painted house clung
to the hill, its windows flashing in the light. I sank, panting,
into a chair on the wide verandah, unable to speak, my eyes
bewitched by the sight before me.

Desmond had flung seed to the soil with a lovely abandon
and the result was a swathe of startling colour that covered the
hillside from the house to the edge of the woods. A white goat
was tethered nearby and a stubby procession of small pigs came
pattering through the riotous flowers like a busy committee of
welcome. One of these snuffed interestedly at my ankles and
Desmond bent to scratch its back.

'Such a pity,' he said, 'that I am so fond of pork. I am
constantly having to replace these little creatures.'

He pushed the pig gently away. 'Now, you must see the
house. The light will be quite perfect.'

Inside the house I caught my breath with pleasure. The large room where we stood had windows on four sides and there was a sense of space and sun and quick air from all the corners of the earth.

I wandered to a window and saw the sea far below, its bays and inlets sparkling between the many islands.

'My peak is a little higher than the others,' said Desmond beside me.

He chuckled. 'It is a constant source of irritation to my British colleagues. You see, in this part of the world, one's standing in the social hierarchy is measured by the height at which one lives. The higher, the greater the prestige and, since the state of my own prestige is questionable, they feel it is somehow wrong that I should be allowed to possess what is possibly the finest view in Hong Kong.' He beamed at me. 'But the reason is, as you have seen, quite a practical one. No roads. Most of the peaks have been stripped bare for fire-wood but until mine reaches that denuded state I shall continue to remain aloof. It's great fun, really.' He pushed me slightly. 'Please, if it doesn't bore you, I'd like to show you the next room.'

I followed him down a short flight of shallow steps into a long room where a Persian rug covered the polished floor and bowls of flowers stood richly on every table. Desmond was watching me and I felt there was something in the room that he especially wanted me to see. Glancing around, my eyes found it almost at once and I knew from the small, satisfied sigh he gave that he had noticed the amazement I was feeling.

'This,' he said in a declamatory voice in which was mixed amusement, 'is my mistress!'

It was a long painting on parchment, a kind of Oriental Madame Recamier, the nude, golden body gracefully arranged on a couch, the eyes watchful and ironic, the lips slightly curved. In the fading light, her skin looked alive and I almost expected her to stir and hold out her hand towards me.

'Who is she?'

Desmond shrugged his shoulders. 'My dear, I don't know.

Some famous courtesan. I found her in a bazaar and bought
her on the spot.' He smiled. 'My students seem a little shocked
by her propinquity, or perhaps they envy me, I'm not sure.'

He stood looking up at the painting for a minute in silence,
his small figure erect, his hands clasped behind his back. Then
he suddenly reached up one hand and flicked the painting
lightly.

'To me she is China.' Then, turning away and rubbing his
hands together, he said in a tone of childish pleasure, 'Now, we
can have tea!'

A few nights later we sat cracking sunflower seeds before the
open fire. The quivering flames accentuated the golden skin of
Desmond's lady and I felt her eyes upon us as we talked.
Desmond wore a blue, embroidered Mandarin coat and when
I complimented him he told me about the last time he had
worn it.

'It was one evening at the Club, I can't imagine why, probably a perverse feeling of curiosity. It was perfectly frightful,
with all that khaki and white drill and the cummerbunds.'

He stared pensively at the fire. 'The poor things. I felt so
sorry for them; they were hideously embarrassed, and they
looked at me as though I had insulted them. Of course, I won't
do it again. One must consider other people's feelings.'

His round face was wistful in the firelight, like a sad child's.
It was an expression I had noticed before on the afternoons
when he came home from work, his thoughts tormented by the
sight of the unhappy refugees who swarmed through the city.

'If only I could help them,' he said to me, clasping his hands
together. 'Money is no good to them. They must be relieved of
their fear and their hopelessness.'

It was on one of these same afternoons that I discovered Ah
Kwong by the back door, ladling out a steaming mixture of
rice and fish to a dozen or more men, women and children,
who held their bowls supplicatingly before them and, receiving
their share, shovelled it hungrily into their mouths. I watched
for a little while before I returned to the verandah where

Desmond was lying on a long chair, contemplating his blazing garden.

'Desmond, who are all these people?'

He looked at me quickly, and I saw the blood rising in his plump cheeks.

'Refugees,' he said off-handedly.

'But how long have you been doing this?'

'Oh, for several weeks. They come every day, but the trouble is I haven't room enough for more than five or six to sleep here.'

'But you must feed dozens.'

'Twenty, thirty, forty, when there are thousands of them . . . What good is that?'

We did not speak of it again.

The day I left Hong Kong, Desmond gave a small party for me at a Russian restaurant in Kowloon. As we drove down to the waterfront, we saw my ship looming in the harbour, an American liner, her sides and decks painted with huge reproductions of the Stars and Stripes.

Desmond looked round at me with his beaming smile.

'My dear, aren't you Americans extraordinary? What a challenge, to advertise your neutrality like that! How long do you think you'll be able to continue?'

The evening passed swiftly. We toasted one another frequently with vodka while the caviar and the blinis vanished from our plates. But my ship sailed at midnight and the moment finally came to say goodbye to Desmond.

He stood up a little tipsily.

'I'll only come as far as the door,' he said. 'Frightful things, farewells. Did you enjoy your blini?'

I looked out across the water, seeing the lights of Hong Kong sparkling up to meet the stars.

'I've enjoyed everything, Desmond.'

I noticed that he seemed restive, as though wishing me to be gone but, with a slightly alcoholic feeling of portending, and because I wished somehow to show my affection for him, I said, 'Desmond, what will you do?'

He looked surprised. 'Do? I shall go back to my peak. What else is there for me to do?'

When the bombs began to fall, and we were all plunged in war, I used to think about Desmond and his peak, wondering if they had escaped destruction. It would have taken a wayward bomb with a delicate slant to render finally to dust that small house half-hidden in the trees.

A year after the war had ended, I learned what happened to my friend. He died in a prison camp, deliberately inviting death by teasing a Japanese sentry into shooting him.

'Of course,' I thought, resisting the pain in my heart, 'Desmond would have loathed the squalor and the desperate unhappiness.'

Although it was improbable, I wished that he might have been wearing his Mandarin coat when he died.

The Long Afternoon

At puberty, pre-puberty and going-on puberty they sat with their backs against a red barn in the dusty sun in the Great West in the summer of '27. A rooster scratched in the earth's powder and there was sleepy, querulous talk between hens. Beyond the thick sage, *piñón* foothills rose to the mountains which, unseen from the barnyard, could still be felt. It was their mystery that impinged, with only a few blazed trails above cattle country and, higher still, on shale slopes, a vantage point where four states, Wyoming, Utah, New Mexico and Colorado—their own state—met according to a manmade diagram. Everything within a hundred square miles was space and past, Indian past. That was part of the mystery. But at thirteen, restlessness began, and thirteen was the leader, Lee by name. The others, Betsy eleven and William ten, followed.

Lee clenched his eyes against the sun. A bluebottle droned and there was a feeling of emptiness in the barnyard as if nothing had happened or ever would. The afternoon was static. He opened his eyes, making blue slits. His eyebrows were bleached almost white by the sun; his close-cut blond hair glistened like tiny wires. The static feeling extended; electricity at rest. He felt within himself an urgency, a swelling power, a need to explode, to shout.

'What'll we do now?'

William was tracing a pattern in the dust with a twig. He liked twigs and sticks and small branches; he and Betsy awaited their leader's decision. They had already visited the boneyard where two dead horses with wide-flung tails like fans sprawled in varying stages of decay. Traps for coyotes were set about the carcasses. The born-dead foal had been examined and seen to

be at the maggot stage, bubbling with corruption. Themselves
still so filled with life, they felt nothing but fascination at the
sight of active death.

'We could go fishing,' said Betsy.

'Too hot. The trout'll be sleeping.' Lee spoke with a certain
satisfaction. A notion of what he would really like to do was
forming in his mind.

'Yeah, it's sure a hot old day.' William drew a wheel, or was
it a tail, on the figure he had created. 'South Pasture's all dried
up.'

Betsy sighed. 'It's the drought. I wonder if the asters will ever
bloom.'

William stopped drawing. He wore his favourite hat, a
Mexican straw sombrero with woollen bobbles hung around
the edge of the brim. 'Daddy says there won't be a second
cutting of alfalfa this year.'

'Who cares?'

Lee spoke roughly, though he adored his small brother. He
was bored with ranch things, with fishing and crops, with cattle
and trails and wilderness. He wanted to be part of life, to bellow
and punch, to be, in the same way, violent!

The corral gate clattered. It was Chick the chore boy, round
Irish face shining with some ambiguous pleasure. He carried a
rifle, pointed downwards, and a large grey goose, its long neck
limp and snakelike in death. Blood tipped its spread wings,
fanned outward from being held upside down—food for the
table.

'You kids playing dirty?'

They chose not to answer. Lee blushed hotly; he could feel
his ears going red. He let a string of saliva fall in clumsy
imitation of spit, the way the cowhands did when squatting on
their hams discussing things. With or without tobacco they did
it. Lee's saliva was contained by dust, but not enough. He
rubbed it hard to make it vanish.

'Don't know what you mean,' he finally said.

But he did, having experimented. He wished he had not said

anything. To avoid Chick and end the encounter, he stood up.
  'Let's get the darned horses then.'
  'Where will we go?'
  'Yeah, where?'
  'Let's go down to the Farm.'
  The Farm was where their foreman lived with his family.
The girls, Blondy and Pearl, were eleven and twelve years old
respectively. Pearl had breasts. They appeared sometimes in
Lee's daydreams, quite often of late. Ten minutes to catch the
horses. There were plenty around. Mr. Webb, their father,
raised horses as well as cattle.
  They chose the fields, though Betsy would have preferred the
road along the foothills. Perhaps they could come back that
way. During the past winter when they moved to town, 250
miles northwest, Mrs. O'Dwyer, the foreman's wife, had given
birth to a baby. Mr. Webb had delivered it because no doctor
could engage the snowdrifts in time to offer professional help.
The baby was dead anyway. That's what they said. Besides,
Betsy was sure her father, whom she had seen deliver foals and
calves and lambs, could deliver a baby too. But there was a
difference. The difference lay in the whole strange sequence of
how the baby got to be there at all. To be sure she knew about,
having watched, the procreation of animals, but this had to be
different. It had something to do with Chick and his 'playing
dirty', though she wasn't sure. She could not make the connection. All she knew, and all she felt with a deep atavistic sorrow,
was that a baby—she had not asked her father whether boy or
girl, could not ask him—lay buried off the trail that led to Ute
Creek. She wanted desperately to visit the grave, now, today.
  But, as was habitual, she followed the leader through the
fields where three times gates had to be opened and closed. Had
it been June, they would have been shutting their mouths
against the clouds of mosquitoes that rose from the thick mixture
of timothy and clover. But the hay had been cut and the mosquitoes were gone until next season. Now the katy-dids made
zipping sounds and grasshoppers flipped among the stubble.

William, being the youngest, opened and shut the gates without grumbling. About to remount, he noticed a small willow branch and picked it up, sticking it in his belt. Shaped like a revolver, it would be just right for their next game of cowboys and outlaws. Bang bang, you're dead! and wooden guns spurting fire, knocking people from their horses. Real guns were not allowed except to shoot prairie dogs and rabbits—vermin, their father said. William had no liking for real guns and blood made him sick. He would rather run than hunt. Run in the foothills until he dropped, his chest hurting, smelling his own sweat. But Lee liked shooting. He seldom missed, either, and had hung dozens of small furry carcasses on the barbed-wire fences as was customary. Those were the prairie dogs and they stayed there until they were dried up, tiny skeletons moving in the slightest breeze.

Betsy too had been given a gun like the others, a .22 Winchester. But after destroying a pregnant rabbit she had stopped shooting, did not even like to think about it.

The O'Dwyers lived beyond the third field. When they were almost there, Betsy moved her horse closer to Lee's.

'Let's go back by the foothills,' she said.

'We'll see.'

He knew about the baby's grave. And he had made the connection but wished he hadn't, feeling disgust at the image of the fat O'Dwyers humping away. What he could not understand was his sister's interest. Girls.

Like the Webbs' house, the O'Dwyers' was built of handmade adobe bricks. But the Webbs' had been painted white, with blue trim on the windows—to keep away the Devil, said the Mexicans—and a red roof. This suggested protocol, boss and employee. But no one thought much about it.

As they were tying their horses to a hitching rail, Blondy came out of the house.

'Come in and set a while,' she said, speaking like her mother.

'Yeah. We got us some iced tea.'

This was Pearl who had short dark hair as well as breasts.

Both she and Blondy wore dresses, unlike Betsy who was mostly clad in blue denim overalls. The O'Dwyers did not ride much. They preferred the mule wagon or the old flivver, a Ford station wagon which sagged on one side because Mr. O'Dwyer, who drove it, was so fat.

'How come you dress so plain?' Pearl had once asked Betsy.

In Betsy's mind, 'dressing plain' became synonymous with not eating chilli. Her father liked chilli, but the O'Dwyers said Mexican food was low-life, like Mexicans.

The iced tea was good. The ice came from a reservoir three miles down the valley. It froze in winter, and big Percherons with caulked shoes were driven out on the ice to haul away huge blocks, sawn from the thick expanse. These were later piled in a building made of cedar logs and covered deeply in sawdust where they remained unmelted for months. On hot days, Lee, though it was forbidden, broached the icehouse door and climbed the sawdust mound to sit in cool ecstasy.

The O'Dwyers borrowed ice. It had not occurred to Mrs. O'Dwyer to make cold drinks until Mrs. Webb suggested it. Today the five children sat in the front room which was really at the back. There was a mail order couch with a Navajo blanket over the seat, and two big chairs, one of which was deeply depressed from Mr. O'Dwyer's weight. Mrs. O'Dwyer, who had a pretty smile, brought the iced tea and chocolate Oreo cookies. Despite her fat, she move lightly.

A silence as deep as the one in the barnyard descended. William took out his 'revolver' and peeled off the bark. Betsy smiled at him. She had seen him pick up the branch. William had been born in a hospital a long way from the ranch. The silences extended. Somewhere, a cow moaned, the sound flattening the day.

'Whatcha want to do?'

Lee seemed to be asking the question of himself for he looked at no one. His gaze was directed towards the fireplace above which hung a deerhead, afternoon sun glinting from dusty glass eyes. Beside it were fixed two long-barrelled shotguns, old, shining. They were Mr. O'Dwyer's treasures; he allowed no one to handle them.

'The reservoir's dried up.'

Pearl was watching Lee who sat with his legs stretched out. He wore corduroy pants and sneakers. He should not be wearing sneakers. There were rules about this. Because of rattlesnakes, they were supposed to wear boots at all times, the lace-up kind. But Lee wanted cowboy boots, black ones embroidered with white butterflies. He had seen some in the Montgomery Ward catalogue.

'How do you know the reservoir's dry?' He did not take his eyes from the guns.

'We rode down in the mule wagon. Papa took the truck to San Luis with a load of wheat. They's fish all over, mostly dead, though some flopped a little. It sure smelled. Pee-ugh!'

'Yeah, and the mud was all cracked,' said Blondy.

Lee still stared at the guns on the wall. He raised his arms, cradling an imaginary weapon and swivelled it around to point at Pearl.

'Gottcha!'

She giggled. 'Oh, you. Think you're smart.'

Lee stood up and walked over to look more closely. 'Wouldn't I just love . . .' He reached up.

Pearl said in alarm, 'Don't you touch them guns.'

'Why not?' He was challenging her.

'Papa don't let anybody touch them guns.'

He turned away. 'I didn't say I was going to touch them.'

Betsy knew that expression. And he was getting red right up to the line of cropped hair. He was angry. She feared for him. Then he smiled, showing large white teeth. All the Webbs had good teeth, not brown-stained like many Colorado children. The brown came from drinking water with too much iron in it. The Webbs had been given bottle water to drink when they were small. It could be equated with their roof being painted red, if they'd bothered to think about it.

'Let's go to the barn and catch chipmunks.'

He was looking at Pearl.

'Sure,' she said.

The screendoor banged. 'Mama says chipmunks are dirty,' said Blondy. 'They give you warts.'

Betsy moved her shoulders in unpleasant memory. 'I caught one once by the tail. It came off in my hand.'

'Did you keep it?'

'Of course not. I threw it away.'

Lee climbed the ladder to the loft. Above him Pearl's strong legs showed bare above rolled stockings. He could see up her skirt but tried not to look. They sat down on a bale of hay close together. Lee felt his heart might burst from pounding there and then. He noticed the loose hay in a corner below a window through which sun shone dustily. He could think of no words to bring about the situation he so desired, but was afraid of. Pearl too was silent. Then both spoke together.

'Mama says—'

'Do you like?—'

They laughed and after that were more relaxed. Lee still could not assemble the urges that either forced him to squirm and scratch at random itches or sit in hot, miserable silence, heavily aware of his body but unable to co-ordinate muscle, bloodstream, sense of smell, need to touch. He went on sitting, conscious of bulk, tight trousers, inadequacy. Beside him Pearl sighed and stirred, and said they'd best be getting back to the house.

William sat on the floor lacing his boots. The laces passed alternately behind brass hooks. They took a long time to finish and always made him late for breakfast because he forgot to get up early enough. The Webbs were summoned to breakfast by a melodious Chinese gong, little inverted cups of subtle colours strung on red cord. The O'Dwyers used a big iron triangle which was struck with the spoke of a wagon wheel until it clanged. Whoever did the striking—usually Mrs. O'Dwyer—

would shout at the same time, 'Come and get it before I throw
it out!'

William liked this; he wished his family had an iron triangle.
When he said as much to Blondy she told him he was nuts. But
she was less emphatic than she might have been before the
O'Dwyers got their inside toilets. There had been a period of
envy when the Webbs were the only family with inside toilets.
Everyone in the valley used to come to see how they worked.
But now the O'Dwyers were equal to the Webbs in that area.

'You think Lee's sweet on Pearl?' Blondy was smirking.

Betsy saw the smirk. 'That's silly. Sweet? For Pete's sake!'

'Sweet. Pete. Sweet. Pete,' chanted Blondy.

They began to giggle, then laugh, exciting themselves until
what had been absurd became meaningless and they fell silent.
Then Betsy said, 'Oh, listen.' Music drifted in from somewhere.
'I reckon it's Highpockets out in the bunkhouse, playing his
harmonica.' Betsy hummed, catching the melody. '*With someone
like you, A pal good and true, I'd like to leave it all behind, And go and
find some place that's known to God alone . . .*'

She broke off as William uttered strange sounds, grunts
interspersed with 'Oh, boy, oh, boy, call that singing!'

Betsy continued, paying no heed. '*We'll build a little nest,
Somewhere out in the West, And let the rest of the world go by.*' She
frowned, 'I think I forgot some words.'

William said, 'I know different words.'

They looked at him in surprise as he sang in a thin, sweet
voice. '*We'll build a little still, Behind a little hill, And let the rest of
the world go dry.*'

He listened happily to their laughter then joined in. His
Mexican hat now hung from its cord down his back.

'It's like Papa's still where he made that beer,' said Blondy.
'He had to throw it in the crik when the sheriff come.'

'I remember.'

'Lots of drunken fish,' said William and this started them off
again.

Lee and Pearl returned to the midst of laughter and Lee

asked crossly what was so funny. Then he walked straight to the fireplace and took down one of the guns, lifting it to his shoulder, hefted it, then lifted again. He peered down the barrel.

'Heavy old bugger. Wish I had a target.' He took aim.

'You'd best put that back. Papa doesn't stand for anyone to take his guns. I told you.'

Lee acted as though he hadn't heard Blondy, continuing to aim the big weapon.

'You wouldn't dare,' said Pearl.

'Who says?'

'Lee, put it back.' Betsy was worried.

'Nerts, it's not loaded.'

He swung round and aimed the gun at the opposite wall, a bit to the right of where William sat on the floor. 'Bet this could kill a grizzly.'

'Maybe, but you couldn't hit the side of a barn door,' said Blondy disgustedly.

'Oh, yeah?'

He squinted and took careful aim. The silence shattered under a powerful explosion. A hole appeared in the wall beyond William's head and as they stared in fright, flakes of plaster detached themselves and fell to the floor.

William said in awe, 'I felt it! I felt the bullet go past my head!' He stared with wide eyes at his brother.

'You couldn't've. I—I aimed high.' His voice quivered as he continued with whining resentment. 'It wasn't supposed to be loaded.'

'Papa's going to be mad.' Blondy sounded quite happy.

Lee hung the gun back on the wall, fumbling over the fixtures because his hands were shaking.

'You could have killed me,' said William bemusedly.

Lee forced himself to turn around. Terror of what he might have done caused his voice to shake like his hands.

'Willy—I'm—Willy, I'm sorry. I didn't mean to scare you.'

When no one said anything, he went on defensively and again with the whine bordering on self-pity. 'How was I to know? The gun shouldn't have been loaded. It was an accident.'

'You didn't oughta touch it in the first place,' Blondy prodded. She was examining the hole in the wall. 'What'll Papa say?'

'I keep telling you. It was an accident.' Fear was turning to a general encompassing anger with them, with the world, with himself. 'Oh, come one, let's go.'

Blondy poked a finger into the hole. 'Good thing Mama went to feed the hogs. Anyway, you'll catch it when Papa gets home.'

'Shut your mouth, Blondy.' Pearl went over to stand by Lee. 'We all know it was an accident.'

'That's what I keep saying,' but he did not look at her. 'You kids coming or not?' He managed a semi-grin, this time glancing at Pearl. 'So long. Abyssinia.'

He left the house first, crashing the screen door behind him. More flakes of plaster dropped from the wall.

The others followed but by the time they crossed the yard beneath the ancient cottonwood trees, Lee had already mounted and was galloping up the lane, raising a cloud of dust to float across the fields.

'Goodbye, Pearl. So long, Blondy. I'm sorry.' She smoothed her horse's mane. It felt comforting.

'Yeah, so long,' said William. 'Be seein' ya.' He had not yet learned to say 'Abyssinia', which was fashionable that year.

They set off up the lane after Lee. By the time they reached the road that followed the foothills, he had stopped and was waiting for them by the cattle stile.

'You took your time.'

It was almost the leader speaking, but Betsy noticed he had been crying. She kept a loyal silence about the fact, but he knew she had seen. He reined his horse in the direction of the home ranch and Betsy rode beside him, William trailing in the rear. The silence between Lee and Betsy was charged, extending painfully until Lee said with a burst, 'I'll take you to see the grave if you like.'

She looked at him, frowning. 'No, I don't want to go.'

She wasn't sure why she felt this way. There didn't seem any magic any more. Perhaps it would come back. They rode on, in renewed silence. It was the time of day when rabbits came out to feed. She would never shoot a gun again, ever. Lee saw some rabbits scamper into the sage and felt repulsion. He would gladly have killed them.

Except where reddish gravel from the *piñón* slopes had sifted down, the road was deep in a white dust, puffing up under the horses' hoofs. The air had the stillness of approaching sunset. A bluejay screamed; meadowlarks lilted on distant fenceposts; somewhere a deer coughed.

William broke his willow stick gun into two pieces. They would do to sail down the stream and under the bridge. He liked waiting for them to appear. Sometimes they were caught in the milky spume accumulating near the bank. He would pick them out and throw them back in the current again.

Betsy said, 'You could have killed William.'

'But I didn't. Heck! I keep saying it was an accident.'

'I'll have to tell—about William.'

'Why? No one's going to ask you.'

She looked down at the cantle of her saddle. Lee glanced at her, then said violently, 'Go ahead, tell.'

'Mr. O'Dwyer will speak to Dad anyway when he finds out.'

'And Blondy will tell,' he added viciously; then, as if ashamed, said in a quieter voice, 'I suppose she'll have to.'

Without looking at him, Betsy said, 'You were showing off, weren't you?'

'Oh, shut up. You're a fool.'

She ignored the anger, concentrating on the part of his voice that she knew from experience meant that he was trying again not to cry.

'Yes, you were. You wanted Pearl to think you're a big shot.'

'Shut up.'

'Blondy says you're sweet on Pearl.'

'Blondy would say anything.'

Now she saw tears in his eyes and put out her hand, laying

it on his, the one that held the saddlehorn, lightly, of course, showing sympathy more than support. Whatever happened or did not happen belonged to the secret area of his life, like the baby's grave.

'I don't expect it matters, Lee. Nobody got hurt.'

'Yeah, that was lucky.' Then he smiled. 'Gee, that old gun was heavy. You just wouldn't believe how heavy it was.'

'I'll bet.'

William listened to them vaguely, noticing how the shadow of the horses' hoofs on the road looked like huge upside-down bottles in the lowering sun.

Incident at Lima Junction

Not one of the three Dorans had ever seen a private Pullman car until that afternoon in June 1929 when they converged upon *The Wanderer* in Buffalo. Mr. Staples, an agent from the railroad line, accompanied them. He thought the Dorans nice-looking kids, the girl especially, but resented their apparent wealth and his capacity as escort. Still, it made a change. He guided them across a succession of tracks that gleamed lonesomely in the sun.

'It's over there behind that roundhouse,' he said, and pointed beyond the shimmering pattern of rails. Signals drooped like flags on a windless day. Somewhere a whistle screamed several times. A switch engine, he thought automatically.

The Dorans followed Mr. Staples in silence, stepping over ties and tracks, crunching cinders. Jonny broke from the group to run along a rail, his arms outspread for balance—like a bird, Sue thought, and imagined him dipping and soaring above the city until he fell or hit a telegraph wire.

'Come back!' called Jamie in disgusted, older brother tones. 'There might be a train.'

'Not much traffic since the Depression,' said Mr. Staples, but watched disapprovingly.

Jonny returned. His dark curls were damp with sweat. He smoothed them self-consciously and looked into the distance.

They walked on, a tidy little phalanx in the big yard that smelled of hot tar, steel and train smoke.

Sue plucked at the sleeve of Jamie's seersucker jacket.

'I wonder what it's like?'

'Like any other Pullman,' he said.

'I think you'll find a lot of different features,' said Mr. Staples.

Rich kids. They take so much for granted. With a multi-millionaire uncle like Wilson Baines in the family, they would never have to worry about problems involving life-insurance, fear of losing jobs, doctors' bills and rent.

'How long will it take to get to California?' Jonny asked.

'Five or six days, depending on what trains will pick you up. Maybe longer.'

'Heck, I thought a private car was fast.'

Sue laughed. Despite resentment, Mr. Staples thought the laugh a pleasant sound. He would have liked a daughter, but had no children.

'Dope!' said Jamie. 'It's not an aeroplane.' He took off his jacket and jerked loose his tie.

Mr. Staples was immediately offended by his sagging paunch and rounded shoulders—a big young fellow. The best steaks, the best butter, Grade-A milk and eggs had gone into that body.

'I'm afraid a private car doesn't rate special privileges. On the line, it's kind of a nuisance.'

He was ashamed of his own sourness, noticing the girl glance at him. Although a blonde, surprisingly her eyes were hazel. The bigger boy was blond too, but he had blue eyes and his hair, in Mr. Staples' opinion, was cut too short, almost like a convict's.

'Not that it isn't very comfortable,' he amended, 'Like a little house on wheels.'

'I can't wait to see it.' The girl's smile delighted him.

'You will in a moment. It's just beyond these locomotives.'

They paused beside three big engines, which were panting one behind the other in the sun.

'Gee, I'd like to ride in one,' said Jonny.

A round, red face appeared in the cab of the first engine. 'Why not, sonny? We've got nothing else to do.'

The engineer wore a peaked cap and leaned comfortably on the cab, his striped-denim arms crossed before him.

'I see you've got your hands full, Jeff,' he said to Mr. Staples and grinned down at Sue. 'Hello, there.'

'Can we, Jamie?' Jonny deferred to authority.

'Be a sport.'

'Later. We ought to go on board first.'

'Plenty of time,' said Mr. Staples.

Jonny, anticipating refusal, had gone to investigate a handcar standing nearby on a short empty stretch of track.

'You don't want one of them,' called the engineer. 'That's for gandy-dancers.'

Jonny came back and for a static moment they all stood looking up at the engine, feeling diminished by the great wheels and pistons, the sheer bulk. The engineer grinned and pointed at Jonny.

'You'll get them ice-cream pants all dirty.'

Jonny glanced down at his white line plus-fours. 'Who cares?' He had flushed deeply.

'Well, if you're going, hurry up,' said Jamie.

As Jonny climbed up into the cab a second man appeared, wiping his hands on snarls of cotton waste.

'What's all this?'

'Passengers for *The Wanderer*,' said Mr. Staples, adding, 'You be careful now,' as Jonny's face appeared in the cab window.

'I'll go with him,' said Jamie.

Mr. Staples hoped he was not exceeding his duties. Instructions had been to stay with the three of them until a train picked up the private Pullman around five o'clock. This was as good a way as any to kill time. It was not the kind of assignment he liked. He took off his straw hat and fanned himself. Sue noticed a tuft of grey hair poking up from the crown of his head and decided he was a kind man and probably good to his children.

'You must be pretty excited, going out to California.' He meant to be sympathetic, but some of his envy leaked out as he added, 'I've never had the money for a trip, much less private cars.'

She seemed surprised. 'I don't think we're really rich, not like Uncle Wilson, I mean. I think—' she hesitated—'I think my father has some business problems.'

Mr. Staples nodded. 'The Depression. It's taken the stuffing out of people.'

The engine blew a blast and they heard the steam come up. As the huge machine huffed away, Jonny, attractively wreathed in vapour, leaned out to wave.

'That little brother of yours is a lively one.'

'Jonny?' She smiled. 'He's fifteen. It's just that he's small for his age.' She looked after the receding engine. 'Will they go far? I'd like to see *The Wanderer*. And my feet hurt. New shoes.'

He glanced down at her feet. Black and white. Spaldings, for sure. Expensive.

'They'll probably backtrack in a minute.'

'That's good. I'd like to take off my shoes. Barefoot's best.'

Mr. Staples had never met anyone like her. Girls he knew did not think of going barefoot. He changed the subject.

'They say California is a pretty place.'

'Yes. I've never seen oranges growing.'

For a moment they both contemplated the pleasant thought of orange trees, then Mr. Staples asked her how old she was. Maybe seventeen?

'Oh, no; I'm just fourteen.'

'Well, now. I thought you were older, a big girl like you.'

To his horror he realised he had winked at her, and hoped she understood he meant no harm. But Sue saw nothing in the wink save amused collusion over the way in which she was fooling the world.

'Yes, I'm tall for my age.'

'Your other brother is a big fellow. Does he play football?'

'Sometimes, I think. I know he likes keeping fit. He goes to Yale.'

'Is that so? Yale College. Well.'

Some of his original resentment returned.

The engine came clunking back, subsiding with a final belch of steam as the boys climbed out. Jonny was excited; Jamie looked tense, wondering whether or not to offer a tip. He did nothing.

The Wanderer was everything they had hoped for with its neat rooms, real beds instead of berths, comfortable armchairs, showers and carpeting. Someone had set bowls of flowers about the place.

They were met by a small Filipino in a steward's white jacket who hopped from the portable steps and bowed.

'Your bags have arrived, but quick. Now you. Welcome.'

'Hello, Ramon.' Mr. Staples slapped him patronisingly on the shoulder.

They made a tour of inspection, admiring the dining room with its big mahogany table where, said Mr. Staples (imagining briefcases stuffed with gilt-edged bonds), their uncle sometimes held business conferences. Jamie wrestled with a problem. Should he invite Mr. Staples to have a drink? Uncle Wilson had a bootlegger. There must be hooch somewhere around. Ramon, when questioned, said this was indeed true and Jamie turned to Mr. Staples.

'Would you like a drink, sir?'

Charmed by the 'sir'—he could not remember that anyone had ever thus addressed him—Mr. Staples accepted and soon they were relaxing in soft chairs, lapping icy liquid. Mr. Staples savoured his Tom Collins, entranced by the idea of drinking some of Wilson Barnes's private stock. The others had lemonade. The Pullman smelled of furniture polish, the fan whirled, but outside all they could see were the distant, sullen buildings of the city.

Under the influence of a second Tom Collins, Mr. Staples gazed fondly at his hosts. Nice kids, not just rich kids. He raised his glass. 'Here's to a happy trip,' and knew as he spoke that he was more than a little drunk.

There was a thump and *The Wanderer* shuddered. Mr. Staples got up from his chair. My God! The switch engine. Time to be going. On the observation platform, he gripped Jamie's hand.

'A pleasure. A real pleasure.' He patted Jonny's shoulder.

'Good boy. Good boy.'

To Sue he behave with deference, but held her hand too long.

'Take good care of her, boysh.'

Knowing his tongue had betrayed him, he almost fell down the steps, prevented by Ramon. As *The Wanderer* moved off down the track, he stood, teetering and waving and calling something.

'Did he say "bum voyage"?' Jonny asked.

'He's boiled as an owl,' said Jamie.

'Poor Mr. Staples. He was enjoying himself.'

Then they forgot him, aware their expedition had begun. *The Wanderer* creaked and oscillated, come suddenly to life. There was excitement in the clashing squeak of couplings and the grinding of the wheels.

'Hurrah!' they said, and 'Oh, boy! We're off!' and of course, 'California, here we come!'

An hour later *The Wanderer* was rocking along, the last car of a St. Louis train headed west.

At first the sense of adventure held. But progress across the continent was slow. Fast trains, as Mr. Staples predicted, did not like hauling a private Pullman. Jonny complained.

'If Uncle Wilson owns the railroad, we should have special treatment.'

'He doesn't own the railroad, just this car,' Jamie said. 'Use your bean.'

The train was trundling across Kansas. Shadow of engine smoke leapt the draws and, in the mute solitude, distant wind-mills turned in the clean, dry air. Bored, Jonny forced the others to play games which he invented. They counted the number of black cars going west; the number of coloured cars going east. They bet each other as to which could see the largest number of cows at a given time. Refinements were added, with black and white cows counting more than red ones. Anyone who saw a bull won the game.

This then palled too, and he tried to make them join him

in song: 'Forty-Nine Bottles', 'Clementine', 'Button Up Your Overcoat'. His repertoire was large. To his whistled accompaniment, he tap-danced up the corridor and tried to draw Ramon, remote in his little kitchen, into a card game. Ramon would not be drawn, though his refusal was pleasantly framed. He had long ago taught himself to simulate, and was never happier than when he could genuinely feel the affability which Americans attributed to ignorance and race, and which he practised now because it was expected of him.

It was Ramon who helped to clarify a troubling phenomenon. Several times, when the train stopped for water in small wayside stations, overalled men on ladders peered at them through the windows which were eventually cleaned. Not, however, before a pantomime of jeers and pointing and silent mouthing.

'Maintenance men,' Ramon said.

'Why are they making crazy faces?' Jonny asked.

Ramon looked embarrassed, but Jamie said firmly, 'Jerks! They're jealous.'

The next time it happened, Jonny, caught in a leering regard, rushed to his room, drew the blinds and lay down on the floor where Sue found him.

'What on earth are you doing?'

'I'm not going to be stared at that way. I wish the train would take off.'

His voice, an adolescent contralto, cracked into girlish treble, and he glared as though the fault were his sister's.

He seemed to have forgotten it when, on the fourth day, the train slowed and a crossing bell jangled.

'Salinas,' announced Ramon. 'We take on ice.'

During the afternoon, mountains appeared, a faint bruise on the horizon. By dinnertime, they had assumed shape and the children moved from side to side of the car as the track curved, keeping the range in view. Each at his window, they watched in silent awe.

They lingered until darkness came, then took their seats when Ramon announced dinner. There were lamb chops dressed up in paper frills, scalloped potatoes and French beans; the hot rolls were wrapped in a napkin and the butter melted as it was spread.

Passing ice cream, Ramon said they would be spending the night on a siding in Lima Junction, Colorado.

'Trout for breakfast. Fresh.' And he beamed at them.

The train rejected them at Lima Junction and went on its way. They sat looking out at the yard, lit by a full moon. It was deserted, save for a few freight cars.

'Let's take a walk,' said Jamie.

Outside, the air was fragrant with sage. They felt the presence of the mountains. Wanting a better view, they followed the tracks as far as the water tower, then in its shadow saw a group of men.

They stopped, not sure whether to go forward or turn back. Someone in the group moved, a displacement of shadow. Someone else began to whistle softly, then abruptly stopped. The silence extended, making the shadows, jet in the moonlight, seem ominous.

A voice said, 'How about giving us a lift?' and there was laughter.

'What about a job?' asked someone else.

'Yeah, what about that?' This time several voices.

'How come your old man's so rich?'

'You going to ask us in for tea?'

The laughter was derisive. But no one moved, and in their immobility there was a threat.

'Let's get out of here,' said Jamie

Feeling exposed and in danger, they walked quickly back down the platform, expecting catcalls; but the men were silent.

Nearing *The Wanderer*, they passed a freight car. Beside it stood a dim figure that moved forward into their path. They stopped uncertainly. The man seemed huge, though he was not much taller than Jamie. He was hatless and bald; in the moonlight his eyes were black holes in his face.

'Excuse me,' he said quietly. 'You got some food for a hungry man?'

'Of course,' said Sue. 'Jamie, couldn't we . . .?'

But Jamie had already taken some coins from his pocket. One fell to the ground as he thrust his hand towards the man, who was shaking his head. 'I didn't ask for money. I'm not a beggar.'

Excited, wanting to be part of it, Jonny said: 'You asked for food. That's begging.'

The man grabbed Jonny's arms, holding him fast. 'I told you, I'm no beggar!' He shook the boy who wriggled and twisted, kicking out hard. 'Son of a bitch!' the man said furiously.

'Let him go,' Jamie shouted, 'or I'll . . .'

'You'll what?'

But he released Jonny and stood confronting Jamie who could think of nothing to say. He was very frightened. Behind him someone said, 'They're just kids, Maloney,' and another added, 'Yeah, take it easy. You want the bulls to come.'

There were half a dozen men now, and one said, 'Beat it, before you get in trouble.'

The walk back to *The Wanderer* was made in silence. Ramon waited by the steps.

'Is trouble?' he asked anxiously.

Once aboard, Jamie told the others to go to bed, and asked Ramon to make coffee.

'Make sure your blinds are down,' he called as Jonny and Sue went off. He was not certain what to do, but felt comforted by Ramon's presence.

'I don't think they'll do anything now,' he said uncertainly.

Ramon shrugged, got up and turned out the lights. Jamie lifted the blind and peered out. The men were still there. A dull confusion of voices penetrated the thick double glass of the window and they saw a man with a lantern who seemed to be disputing with the others.

'Night watchman,' said Ramon. 'He tell them go. They will

not go. They wait for early morning freight and ride rods.'

The night watchman left. Perhaps, Jamie thought, this happened every night. Ramon fell asleep and snored. Jamie sat
tensely, trying to understand what had happened. He knew
about the Great Depression and that because of it his father
was in financial trouble. He understood poverty was an enemy
though he had not considered it in relation to himself. In New
York, he had seen men selling apples on the street, and always
gave them money, though he would not take the fruit he'd
bought. He did not like apples much anyway. The miserable
faces and shabby clothes embarrassed him. Like the man
tonight, they looked at him with dislike or a sad irony. They
thought him better off than they. Well, he probably was. That's
the way things were.

A train mourned from afar. He looked out to see the moon
had waned. The train mourned again, and now he saw that
what he thought was distant had already emerged from the
darkness in a great bullseye of light and the sound of pistons.
He caught a glimpse of two men in the headlight's glare and
then the freighter rolled past, car after car, moving slowly.

Ramon woke up and peered into the gloom.

'They will go now.'

'Where?'

'Oh, California, maybe. Oregon. Try to work in lumber
camps. Or pick fruit. Anything. Then maybe come back here;
work in harvest. June is no good time for work. No month any
good these days.'

'How do you know all this?'

'I know,' Ramon said gently.

The freighter's caboose went past, its red tail-light swinging.
It vanished, and soon there was nothing more to hear or see.
The stretch of track was quite deserted.

'You go to bed, Ramon.'

Jamie sat on. He felt lonely and imagined Maloney and his
friends clinging to the rods, or sitting with their knees drawn
up in empty freight cars. Then he straightened in his chair as

a sound came from the observation platform. He considered calling Ramon, then collected his courage and opened the door. A man stood there, urinating. Jamie listened to the splash with outrage.

'What the hell!'

The man turned. It was Maloney. He was buttoning his trousers. 'That's what I think of your charity, kid.'

Jamie rushed at him, hitting out hard enough to cause Maloney to lose his balance and fall from the platform. Somehow, the bastard had forced open the little gate that Ramond should have locked. Jamie stood looking down, suddenly terrified. Suppose Maloney was seriously hurt. But after a moment, he stood up and without looking back, limped away just as another freight train crashed through.

Jamie did not go to bed, restless and deeply humiliated by what had happened. Soon after dawn, he took a bucket of water from Ramon's kitchen and sluiced down the platform. Setting down the bucket, he watched the day arrive. It was quiet out there, except for a meadowlark lilting on a fencepost. He smelled wild clover. The sun rose, bleaching away the shadows. Nothing moved, until a truck appeared, bouncing along the dirt road that probably led to a town. He picked up the bucket and went inside. Jonny and Sue must never know about Maloney's visit.

In Albuquerque, New Mexico, the train to which *The Wanderer* was attached stopped, as was the custom, for half an hour so the passengers could inspect the Indian wares spread out along the platform: jewellery, baskets, leather goods, handmade by the Navahos who crouched against the station wall. Jonny and Sue went off to buy souvenirs, but Jamie did not join them, and was alone when a heavy-set man in a pale grey suit, blue tie and grey hat, came aboard. He walked quietly, startling Jamie.

'My name's Benbow,' he said. 'Lieutenant Benbow. Railroad police.' He took off his hat but did not extend a hand.

'You in charge here?'

'I suppose so.' Jamie's thoughts panicked. Had it anything

to do with Lima Junction and Maloney? Not waiting to be asked, Benbow sat down, putting his hat on a neighbouring chair.

'What's your name?'

He consulted a typed sheet of paper as Jamie said, 'Jamie Doran'.

'Yeah, that's right. You're the one. There's a couple of kids too, it says here. Where are they?'

'My brother and sister. They're buying souvenirs.'

'Souvenirs,' Benbow repeated in a negative tone. His broad face was expressionless, but Jamie found something familiar about the high cheekbones and deep-set black eyes. His hair was black and glossy. He glanced around the room.

'Pretty snug. I wouldn't mind having one myself.' He turned back to Jamie. 'Well, I suppose you're wondering why I'm here.'

'Yes.'

'I want to ask a few questions. First: you know a man called Jeff Staples?'

'He's the agent for my uncle's company. He showed us to the car at Buffalo.'

'That's right. Well, he's dead. Got hit by a caboose when he was leaving the yard.' He watched Jamie's shocked reaction closely. 'Yeah. Died right away.'

'That's terrible.' He was remembering Mr. Staples waving drunkenly. Sorrow touched him, then gave way to fear. Mr. Benbow leaned forward.

'Was he crocked?'

Jamie said uneasily. 'He had a drink.'

'Don't give me that. He was crocked.' He looked around the car. 'Where do you keep it?'

Jamie pointed to the cabinet. 'It's locked. Ramon keeps the key.'

'Ramon? That the steward? I better talk to him.'

He got up, leaving Jamie wondering unhappily why he hadn't stopped to think they were breaking the law in giving

Mr. Staples a drink. But everyone broke the law.

Ramon saw Benbow in the kitchen doorway and hid his nervousness with a polite bow. He smiled ingratiatingly, recognising police. A man like this had picked him up once in LA for nothing. Had his latest graft been found out? As he talked to Benbow, verifying the fact that Mr. Staples had had two drinks, he studied the man's face and his manner grew more offhand, though he opened the cabinet without comment and took out the gin. Benbow turned the bottle carefully round, reading the label. He unscrewed the cap, sniffed, inhaled, then looked at Janie.

'It smells like the real stuff all right. English. Must be straight off the boat.'

He sounded quite genial. Jamie realised that he was meant to offer the lieutenant a drink, which justified his previous thoughts. The law itself breaks the law. Benbow accepted.

'I don't say no to the real stuff. It's the rotgut that isn't worth the trouble.'

As Ramon, deliberately inscrutable, went off to fetch the makings, Benbow sat down, hitched up his pants and leaned back comfortably. Jamie asked him what would happen now.

'I mean, I feel sort of responsible.'

'You're goddamn right you are.'

'Does that mean you're going to arrest me?'

'Maybe.'

Jamie again saw Maloney's body thudding to the ground. Benbow was gazing round the room. 'It must cost a lost to operate a thing like this.'

'I never thought about it.'

To Jamie's relief Ramon returned with the drinks. He left the bottle on the table, not looking at Benbow. The latter drank, blew an exaggerated breath and felt his stomach.

'That's what I call a drink. Never had a Tom Collins before.'

Jamie listened, despising the man. 'If there's anything I should do, like get in touch with my uncle, you'd better tell me. I feel terrible about Mr. Staples. Drinking's against the law.'

He paused before the dilemma and for the first time Benbow smiled.

'I know what you're thinking and I don't hold it against you. Maybe I am stepping out of line as a police officer. But the way I see it there shouldn't be any Prohibition. Drinking's human; I'm human, so I take a snort now and then.'

'Would you like another?'

Holding his second drink, Benbow said quietly, 'Maybe Staples had an accident.' He paused. 'Like the guy at Lima Junction.'

'You know about him!' Jamie stood up. 'I'd better telegraph my father before the train leaves.'

He could no longer suppress the panic.

Maloney must have been hurt—maybe killed like Mr. Staples!

'Sit down. There's no call for that.' He finished his drink and picked up the bottle lovingly. 'The real stuff.'

'Would you like the bottle?' Jamie asked despairingly. 'My uncle wouldn't mind.'

'Watch it,' said Benbow. 'Not that I wouldn't guess he has a case or two stashed away. No, I wouldn't take a bottle. I'll just take what's left.' He took a flask from his hip pocket and poured the rest of the gin into it. 'Destroying the evidence, you might say.' He looked at Jamie. 'Maloney's a bum.'

Jamie, still awaiting the worst, stared at his visitor. 'You mean he wasn't hurt—he's okay?'

'Sure. Scum like that always saves themselves.' He finished his drink and set down the empty glass. 'Still and all, you gotta lay off hitting people. Big young guy like you. Could hurt a man who hasn't been eating.'

Relief utterly silenced Jamie. Benbow appeared not to notice, but stood up and started towards the door. He turned back. 'Staples had diabetes,' he said casually. 'He wasn't supposed to drink, not unless he had the right amount of insulin. He must have slipped up that day.'

'Then it was an accident! But you said . . .'

Benbow seemed to be enjoying Jamie's anger.

'I said it was an accident and I'm investigating the case.' He patted his back pocket. 'We understand each other, don't we? No one around here saw me take a drink and Staples sure as hell had an accident.' He bent to peer out a window. 'Those two over there your brother and sister? That girl with the blonde hair and the kid?'

Jamie looked. 'Yes.'

Why couldn't the guy just leave!

But Benbow was still looking. 'Noble Redskins,' he said sarcastically. 'They squat on their hunkers all day long, selling phoney junk and living off the government. It's taking the bread from the mouths of decent Americans. What the hell they got reservations for?' He straightened up and glanced at Jamie with an odd smile. 'Or so they tell me.'

At the door he paused again. 'Take it easy, and tell that Flip back there to keep his yap shut.'

Watching from the window, Jamie saw Benbow walking along the platform. He did not turn his head as he passed the Indian pedlars.

Behind Jamie, Ramon said, 'I think he is Redskin like I am Flip.' There was animosity in his voice.

He walked off, white jacket militarily straight. Jamie thought about his remark. That would be why Benbow's face seemed familiar. Instead of a grey felt hat, he could have been wearing feathers.

It was Jonny who wore the feathers as he and Sue returned to *The Wanderer*, hot and pleased with themselves. It was a splendidly coloured chieftain's headdress, its plumes flopping around his young face and down his back. Easy tears came to Sue's eyes when Jamie told her about Mr. Staples; Jonny screwed up his features in one of his special expressions and went out to sit on the platform, still wearing the headdress. Jamie joined him as the train began to move at last. The outskirts of Albuquerque slipped by and they were in the open desert.

'Look!' Jamie pointed to where an Indian on a bony, black horse raced through the tall cactus and rabbit brush.

'Come on!' yelled Jonny, but the Indian had already dropped behind as the train gathered speed.

Jonny slumped back in his chair. 'I'm a ding-dong Daddy,' he chanted, then fell silent. Suddenly he snatched his headdress off and threw it over the railing. It fluttered and settled on the track. In a moment it had vanished.

'Why'd you do that?' asked Jamie. 'You'll probably never get another one.'

'What's the diff?' Jonny shrugged. 'It was just a bunch of feathers.'

The Federal Agents are Coming

As children growing up in Colorado during the Prohibition era, my brothers and I were given every opportunity to learn the mass deception practised by our elders with regard to what are still called alcoholic beverages. Too young for the furtive knock, the eye at the speakeasy grill, or the gin-filled teacup, hastily hidden, we nevertheless had a warm acquaintance with this negative social experiment, beginning and ending on the wrong side of the law.

In Colorado Springs, where we spent the winters and went to school, the smell of juniper berries crept through the house, while frequent visits of a small, genial man with a large suitcase became as familiar a part of our lives as visits from the iceman and his wagon.

The small man first introduced himself as a cereal salesman, but we heard denial in the clinking sounds issuing from his heavy case. He always came at dusk, parking his car a block down the street. My father would admit him and take him to the study where they would shut themselves in for fifteen minutes or so. Those were the evenings when our father emerged with an extra sparkle in his eye, and we soon discovered that the expression, 'straight off the boat' offered with a happy rubbing of hands, was synonymous with a general atmosphere of great good humour. Now, of course, I know illegal bottles of real Scotch whisky had reached at least one destination. The small man was a bootlegger.

On our ranch in the Sangre de Cristo mountains, the merry breaking of the law continued. Halcyon summers were fraught with sounds like pistol shots as stoppers exploded from bottles of home-made beer. The air in the tractor shed down by the creek was charged with fumes from a brew of locally grown hops and yeast; and in the sheep pasture rose the mound of a small earth cellar, sprouting weeds and heavily insulated against intrusion or discovery by thick bushes and padlocked door. The contents of this cellar were simply known as 'pre-war' and used sparingly.

It seemed inevitable that this criminals' paradise must be invaded, and one warm August day the first whisper of disaster came from our valley.

Harve Shannon, our foreman, brought the news. He had driven to Fort Garland (population 300) nine miles away to bring back the mail, supplies and, for us, a box of chocolate-covered cherries and a bag of red-hots.

We waited for him, lolling on the ragged spread of grass that passed for a lawn. Soon the familiar cloud of dust appeared below the *piñón* knolls. We knew every dip and hill, which we called 'thank-you-ma'ms', and could accurately forecast the time it would take until we heard the clink and rumble of the cattle stile and the last hollow thump as the Model-T station-wagon crossed the wooden bridge. This elderly car had become Harve's means of conveyance ever since, an enormous six feet six, he had grown too fat to ride a horse anything less than Trojan. Under his weight, the springs had fractured one by one, and the flivver canted drunkenly to the driving side. As he drew up in a hullaballoo of brakes we heard in the ensuing silence the water boiling in the engine and knew with pleasure that the potato he used as a radiator cap would be cooked to a turn.

We crowded around expectantly, but he rose up, an unsmiling, red-faced Gulliver and dismissed the pygmies.

'The Feds are coming,' he said fiercely and stomped off to find our father, looking top-heavy in the white, high-heeled, embossed boots he still persisted in wearing. Though puzzled, we let him go, and turned our attention to the flivver; no box of chocolates, no red-hots, no supplies. And the mailbag was empty. We had worked for the candy, cutting brush and cleaning stalls. Indignantly we hurried after Harve to demand an explanation.

We got nothing, either from our father or from Harve. Instead, we were told to saddle our horses, get the hell out to the southside of the valley and pick wild asters. We grumpily obeyed. Who wanted flowers during what appeared to be a crisis? And what were Feds?

The expedition proved more satisfactory than we expected. We returned as the sun began to drop low over the mountains; dripping flowers, we walked up from the stables, and by the tractor shed saw a most extraordinary sight.

Juan Roybal, the Mexican cowhand, was driving a mixed huddle of horses, cows and sheep in frenzied circles near the gate leading to the sheep pasture. Horns clashed, udders swung, brown and amber eyeballs rolled in pained astonishment. The noise and dust were of the stockyards. As we stared, our father appeared in the wide door of the tractor shed. He advanced to meet us, rubbing his hands. His Stetson was crooked and we realised the smile he offered us to be indubitably one of the 'straight-off-the-boat' variety.

'They'll never find it now,' he said, and explained the reason for this madness.

In Fort Garland, Harve had learned the Federal agents were sweeping through Costilla County ('Home of Pigs, Peas and Prosperity' read the welcoming sign), leaving despondency behind and evoking alarm before arrival. They had been in Alamosa that morning and, rumour had it, were due to reach Fort Garland at any moment. This meant they would visit all the ranches in the area, sniffing out the secret stills behind the barns and in the woods, confiscating man's small, bottled joys, and sending us all, we decided excitedly, to jail. Pioneers holding back hostile Indians at the battle of Wagon Wheel Gap had nothing on us now. We were protagonists in a real-life drama.

What had been done by way of preparation for this siege? Our father had a partial answer to this question. All random bottles kept in the house had been removed and taken to the earth cellar. Juan's flourished stick and Mexican invective kept the farm animals circulating so their hoof prints would replace the tyre marks of the truck that had carried the contraband to safety. But there remained a problem: the barrels of mash and the rows of bottles in the tractor shed. There was no room for these in the cellar. It was largely Harve's dilemma, for this summer it was he who had grown the hops, brooded tenderly over the barrels and bottled what was ready. Beer for Harve meant a glow of warmth throughout the long, snow-bound winter evenings, a glow far surpassing that of the portly Franklin stove.

What could be done? Time was running out; the stern pundits of law and order would soon be here.

Harve, emerging from behind our father, had plainly already resorted for inspiration to the contents of more than one beloved bottle. His hat was gone, his bald dome and face poured with sweat. There was a demented gleam in his blue Irish eyes.

'It's evidence the bastards want. I'll fix it so's there won't be none. All they'll find will be a stink.'

He brought an armful of gurgling bottles from the shed, hugging them against his chest. We watched in amazement as he wove and teetered to the creek's edge.

'Better them than me,' he said, and heaved a bottle.

It broke against the rocks beneath the shallow, purling water. He threw another and another, while we stood dumbfounded. The bottles flew through the air, gleaming and shattered. Beer and pure mountain water mingled. We spoke of drunken fish. Another load was fetched, and then another. But no one moved to help him. This was Harve's private war, his battle against man's betrayal of his better self. The Black and Tans marched up the valley. Continuing sound of breaking glass; the smell of beer; his profanity delighted us.

Now came the moment for the barrels: grunt and heave. My father, Juan and Harve rolled the barrels out one by one and tipped their foul-smelling, bubbling contents into the creek.

The resulting mixture looked like gargantuan vomit. We held our noses stating that the fish would die. 'What's a few fish?' said Harve. We thought we understood. He had saved his honour.

Our mother, who had been standing watch, came running down the slope from the garage.

'They're coming! I just saw a dust cloud.' She winced back from the stench, looking from man to man. 'You've been drinking.'

'A final tribute,' said my father.

Harve retrieved his hat and set it firmly on his head. He led the unsteady march; we trailed behind. Unheard martial music filled the air. We held ancient rifles, or were they pikestaffs? No matter. Confontation with the enemy was imminent, no quarter given. I took my father's hand. As we reached the garage, we heard at once the familiar sounds of the stile and bridge vibrating under alien wheels. It was as if the first volley had been fired. We waited. Around the corner of the house came a shabby Dodge truck. The sheriff, Shorty Hoagland!

'What in hell . . . !' said Harve.

In appearance, Shorty Hoagland was scarcely a prepossessing emissary of the law. He made up for his lack of stature by spinning vividly untrue yarns: his limp moustache and dirty woollen waistcoat were always stained by tobacco juice. His small eyes were far brighter than his official badge. We never thought him capable of arresting anybody. Perhaps he never had. Now he took his time getting out of the car as one who knows that all depends on him.

'Where're they at?' demanded Harve.

Shorty did not answer. While we waited, palpitating, he leaned against the truck, took out a slab of Prince Albert tobacco and bit off a corner. His jaw moved tranquilly.

'They ain't acomin'.'

A sound of anguish. We saw Harve deflate before our eyes. The red, excited face creased in sudden woe like a monumental baby's. We thought with awe that he might shed tears.

'They got to come.'

We listened wonderingly as Shorty told us the agents had changed their plans, veering off to Monte Vista and East through the Montezuma Valley. Shorty had no idea why they'd done this. He was watching Harve thoughtfully.

After a pause, he said, 'What goes on in private ain't nothing to do with Feds.' He winked at our father, who looked surprised.

'All my beer,' moaned Harve.

Our father put an arm across the massive, bowed shoulders.

'I've got an idea. Why don't we go on up to the house and have a nip from a bottle of pre-war.' He glanced at Shorty. 'Strictly for medicinal purposes, of course. Will you join us, Shorty?'

'Wouldn't say no.'

They walked away and we did not follow, knowing we were not wanted. The water in the stream seemed to boil below a turgid surface. We swilled it round with sticks, but saw no dead fish—perhaps later. In the morning, Harve seemed as usual and nothing was said about the disaster. But the barrels in the tractor shed fumed no more that summer.

Perilous Seas

It was the night of the Country Club Dance. Not that she had been invited. Not at thirteen. Occasionally she wondered if it was harder to be thirteen in the 1920s than it would have been long ago, when men were gallant and girls had tumbling curls like in those paintings she had been shown at school by a man named Burne-Jones.

Nowadays, in the Twenties, here in her home town of Colorado Springs, there were no curls and in addition a girl was supposed to have a flat chest. Hair was short and shingled, although her sister Cicily kept hers long and puffed it out with gobs of false hair called rats. How foul!

But the puffs did not detract from Cicily's popularity, neither they nor, strangely, a chest that wasn't flat at all. Cora found all this unfair. But she had her own life to consider. Poetry was her refuge against a hostile world. She declaimed it aloud when taking solitary walks in the foothills, her imagination wrenching English idiom to suit the rougher configuration of Western landscape, where there was no season of 'mellow fruitfulness', no 'pale beds of blowing rushes', no King Arthur; and where Wilfred Owen's 'slow drawing-down of blinds' contained a sadness as remote to her as reminiscences of Iwo Jima or Changi to a thirteen-year-old today.

Yet there were moments when poetry failed her briefly. Tonight, for instance, as the house vibrated with preparation, Cicily's bathsalts scented the air and Cicily herself called to Cora to see the results of her visits to the dressmaker. For this Country Club Dance was in costume. Cicily had chosen to go as the Seven Seas. Her dress was sky-blue and hung about with silver cardboard 'C's. Cora had to admit that her sister did look very pretty, and her dress, which was of taffeta, rustled beguilingly.

The doorbell chimed. It was Chuck Farnsworth, come to pick up Cicily, who ran down the stairs on silver feet, a Spanish shawl pulled round her bare shoulders. Cora followed, standing at the door to watch them drive away in Chuck's Flying Cloud. The Country Club was only across the street and they could have walked. But to do so would have been unthinkable, and Cora agreed with this.

She heard the music start up and sought to comfort herself with visions of newly blooming sand lilies on the lower slopes of the foothills. There was a wild rose fragrance in the air of their little suburb, more country than town, and the stars were enormous. Cora felt obscure longings, and poetic metaphor fell from the heavens. Falling stars, falling stars... She hurried upstairs to her room and sat at her white desk, which was locked. 'Private Property. ABSOLUTELY NO ADMIT-TANCE', warned a sign she had printed when aged eleven, and never removed.

Her notebook was bound in pebbled paper and the sheets were rich and creamy. It contained the rendering of nebulous emotions, intangible sexual semaphore, dot-dot-dash, rime royal of desire, combined in a pubescent surge, a need to exteriorise.

'What am I? A plaything of the stars?'

She ceased writing and chewed her pencil.

Behind her chair the room was in darkness—the room where she had in early childhood awakened to fear, where shadow and substance became figures from nightmare, where she had lain frozen in bed, unable even to summon up courage to switch on the light and reveal only familiar furniture and discarded clothing. She stood up and went to the window.

Stillness scattered as a streetcar went clipping past, leaving sparks behind. She watched it affectionately. On Hallowe'en, she and Cicily—when younger—had put a bench across its path, or left buffalo nickles on the rails, rushing later to retrieve them flattened and thin. The streetcar had seats upholstered in straw matting; it always smelled of electricity.

The stillness came back. She missed the streetcar. Suddenly it and the room were a part of nostalgia. She heard laughter from the Country Club and felt angry that she could only listen from afar. Excluded. Fat, thirteen, with an incipient pimple on her nose. She braced herself against these thoughts. Wanting to conform, she swerved away, seeing herself splendidly the leader in a crusade against the Philistines. There was always poetry.

She took out her copy of *The Poetical Works of John Keats* from the row of special books; not enough of them to prevent them from leaning towards or away from one another. One day, they would be tightly packed as wafers, and would include her own published verse.

She read snatches from the Odes. 'La Belle Dame Sans Merci' she knew by heart. Idiots, black and white idiots with their girls—over there, across the street and one block down. Pale and sadly loitering... Odes again. Here was Ruth amid the alien corn. She had never heard a nightingale and its song, charming magic casements, 'opening on the foam/Of perilous seas...'

The doorbell rang.

Because her parents were out and the cook gone to bed, Cora went downstairs. Len Macintosh was the last person she expected. He stood there on the porch looking more like Len Macintosh than Lochinvar, and she was delighted to see him. Len lived in the town, a circumstance that had its snobbish aspects. Her suburb was where the richer people lived, though she was not consciously making comparisons. Tall, quite old really, at least twenty-five, Len had thick blond hair that flamed with Titian tints in the porchlight. His stance was uncertain, his smile wavered. She guessed him to be three sheets in the wind, an expression she had learned from her father.

'There goes Len Macintosh, three sheets in the wind as usual.' She knew the expression to mean having had too much to drink, to be 'under the influence', but in nautical terms it meant nothing to her. Her father constructed small schooners with decks made of cigar boxes, but otherwise they were all land-lubbers.

'Len—how nice of you to call.'

That sounded just like her mother; she was not proud of it.

She told him she was the only member of the family at home, rather surprised that his disappointment should arise from missing her father. She would have thought his interests concerned Cicily. She invited him in.

He looked very big sitting in one of her mother's chintz-covered chairs, his long legs stretched out. He sank a bit, the collar of his tan jacket hitting him just below the ears—neat ears, close to his head. He ruminated, staring down at his hands, large and folded. How long his eyelashes were! There was silence. Pleased by his presence, obscurely excited, she saw them as a pair, abandoned by those who qualified for Country Club dances. She longed to meet him half way to somewhere. Naturally both spoke at once.

'Cicily's at the dance.'

'Is your sister at the dance?'

They both laughed. Rather, she laughed. He exposed his teeth, nice teeth, and said, 'Now ain't that a thing.'

Disqualified, of course for 'ain't'. Her sympathy strengthened. What did he do? What he *did* was always changing: part-time cab driver, filling-station attendant, sometimes nothing at all. Yet he seemed to prosper. How could she amuse him, gain his attention, this handsome man who seemed happy to talk to her, a thirteen-year-old?

Then it occurred to her she must offer him a drink. Coffee? Cocoa? Ginger ale? Rootbeer? A cocktail? She had seen her father shaking up cocktail ingredients, but had no idea of what they consisted, except gin. And the gin was locked away in the 'wine closet' on the upstairs landing. It was a Yale lock, and her father had the key. Sometimes, in the evening, a man would call with a heavy suitcase and her father would take him into the study. She knew him to be the bootlegger and that if he were late it would be time to make gin in the bathtub. She and Cicily were not supposed to understand these things, being sheltered, but the house would be filled with the smell of juniper berries and at times a bottle exploded in the night.

Len Macintosh looked thirsty. She offered him the rootbeer. He accepted, but when she brought him a tall glass of the stuff, he did not drink, only held the glass in one large hand. She felt like saying 'beaded bubbles winking at the brim' but felt it to be unwise. Instead, she told him the rootbeer was homemade and that she and Cicily thought it could make one tipsy if drunk in quantity. He seemed unmoved. Yet a spark of interest showed at the mention of Cicily.

'She gone to the wing-ding over at the Club?'

'Yes. It's a fancy-dress party.'

More silence. He set the glass down on the table by his chair, and she despaired. Then she remembered the bottle of wine in the sideboard—white grapejuice her mother called it when she was small. But neither she nor Cicily had been fooled. If parents or visiting grown-ups drank it, just like the gin it made them laugh more and talk louder, and their mother would start speaking French.

She suggested the wine to Len, stating that it was 'pre-war'. She felt he would know what pre-war meant even if she didn't.

When she returned with a glass of wine, he was screwing back the top of a leather-covered hip flask. Her father had one like it. Len enjoyed the wine, drinking it down quickly.

'French,' he said. 'Gay Paree. You ever been there?'

Flattered, she said she had not travelled very much. She would like to go to Paris, though.

'Me too. But I'll never go nowhere.'

He sounded less sad than resigned. She wanted to give him something to make up for never going to Paris. She wanted to hold his hand.

'When you think your daddy's coming home?'

'Well, they went to a dinner party. It could be late. But you never know.'

He asked if he could wait a bit, and called her honey, at the same time wondering why he wanted to see her father. She felt better than he did. Their twosome was somehow regularised. She could enjoy the situation without fear.

'Would you like to play pontoon?'

He said he only played poker. By now he was speaking in a blurred kind of way, but appeared quite relaxed. She wished desperately to entertain him. When he said he liked to read, she felt encouraged. Not poetry, however.

'I don't go for things like that. I'm stupid.'

The wine, or whatever was in his flask, made havoc of the word 'stupid'.

'You're not. I'm sure you're not. Perhaps you don't know your hidden possibilities.'

He laughed loudly, rather offending her. 'That's rich, that's really rich.' She forgave him everything when he added, 'You're a cute kid.' He leaned forward as he said this and touched her cheek gently. She put up her hand to take his, but he was already drawing back, leaning too much to one side. By now she was fizzing with romantic feelings. She longed to give him something of herself, to confide, to share what mattered most.

'I write poetry.'

'Yeah?'

He had retreated. His legs were again stretched out, his hands folded. There were little gold hairs on his fingers.

'Would you like to hear some?'

'Sure. Fine.'

She closed her ears to the lack of enthusiasm, and hurried upstairs to fetch the poems. She brought the volume of Keats as well. As she entered the drawing-room, he was again screwing on the top of his flask. She ignored this. Pulling her chair closer, so they were toe to toe, she began.

Ten minutes or so passed. She finished a poem called 'Quitting Time' of which she was very proud: 'The workman stretched his arms, stood and spat into the sunset's red/It's quitting time, by God, he said.'

She thought it very daring, very forthright. It balanced her romantic verses, which she also liked enormously.

She looked up expectantly. He was asleep, golden head dropping on chest, hands still folded. He seemed to be utterly vulnerable and beautiful. Endymion. Chained. She sat in fascination. He stirred, opening hazy blue eyes.

'Rea' s'more.'

It was an invitation to dance with her seven veils, to clash cymbals, whirl and turn and do a bellydance. She was his handmaiden, his houri, his slave. She read him Keats's 'Ode to a Nightingale'. By the time she reached 'Oh, for a draught of vintage', he was snoring gently. She put down the book, leaning forward to study his face. His lips were open a fraction, red and youthful, not a 'purple-stained mouth' but she had an urge to kiss it. She had never kissed a man save her father or a relative or two, and never right on the mouth.

She was too shy. Certain he was still soundly sleeping, she went to the front door and opened it. Music from the Country Club sounded louder. She recognised 'Melancholy Baby', a piece she had learned to play on her ukelele. It did not move her. What she was experiencing was of value, not superficial social stuff.

'They're all wet,' she whispered, and turned back to her love.

He was awake. 'Hi, kiddo. Sorry. Fell asleep.'

'Oh, that's all right.'

In sleep he had been hers. Now he would leave her. Instead, to her joy, he invited her to 'take a little ride'.

'I'll bring you back safe, but I've got to be somewhere in half an hour.'

Len's car was an old, quiet, four-door sedan. She did not know the make, nor care. She sat next to him in the front as they sailed past the drive to the Country Club, glancing only briefly at the lights pouring from wide windows. She wondered where they were going, but did not ask. It was enough to be

here beside him, a chosen companion, albeit thirteen. He put
out his hand and pulled her closer so that she had to watch her
feet near the gear-shift. Her heart galloped. She hoped for
further disclosures of the great mystery of love, but after saying,
'That's better', he went back to driving. She sat stiffly, her
shoulder against his arm. It was uncomfortable, but she would
not have changed places with anyone in the world at that
moment. Too aware of his closeness, she did not notice the route
they were taking until the lights of town dropped behind and
she knew they were in the Garden of the Gods, that valley of
rocks that in sunlight are their own Titian red, but in the night
hulked dark and unidentified.

'Got to meet this guy,' Len said, though she had asked no
question.

She could not ask. She wanted this extraordinary incident to
become more than incident, but while it was, she must savour
every minute of it. She was 'on a date'.

They had crossed the valley and were in the hills. She smelled
pines and let it mingle happily with the scent that was Len's,
a clean, manly smell, and the sweetish exhalation of alcohol. If
he had stank, she would have accepted the fact, unshaken.

The car was climbing. Suddenly they stopped. It was black
as Len turned off the headlights.

'Wait a minute, honey. I'll be right back.'

She sat very still, part of the great stillness of the mountains
that enfolded her. No poetry was necessary; this was a poem.
She waited.

Into the silence fell a little sound, the chink of glass, then low
voices, then silence again. A moment later he was back at the
car. He was alone, but moved carefully, displacing shadow with
the faint pallor of his jacket. She lost him, then heard sounds
at the back of the car. He was loading something into the
luggage compartment. A bang, and then he was getting in
beside her. The hint of alcohol had become authoritative. His
voice was low, but excited.

'Okey-doke, we'll go now.'

They drove higher, found a side track, turned and started down the mountain. She knew some transaction had taken place, important to Len. The transaction had involved another man, and bottles. Len was a bootlegger. She had guessed, but it made no difference. He had given her his confidence.

They were in the valley. He stopped the car beside a dull mass of stone. For a moment he did not move, and the car made little ticking sounds as springs settled and the engine cooled.

'Well, I did it,' he said. He turned to her. 'You're a sport.'

She was silent. She did not want to be a sport. She wanted to be his handmaiden, do a bellydance, shake her bobbed hair, hold his hand . . . He put his hand under her chin and she went tense from foot to head. His face was close to hers and then she felt his lips on her mouth, gentle as a butterfly kiss. They became firmer and more demanding. His hand twisted and his lips twisted on hers. The smell of alcohol was overpowering. Abruptly he drew back.

'That's enough.'

As they moved on he asked her name.

'Cora,' she said.

'Well, Cora, we've made a real good evening of it.' She sensed he was too casual when he added, 'Don't let on I kissed you. That's our secret.'

'Yes.'

She wondered if she could not perhaps become a bootlegger's moll, be Len Macintosh's woman. But she was only thirteen, and he had not remembered her name.

The house was still empty when they got back. He leaned over to open the door for her, but did not get out of the car.

'Cora, tell your daddy to get in touch with me.'

'All right.'

Wasn't he going to kiss her again? Had he not understood that she shared her soul with him, her defensive secrets, carefully kept from a hostile world?

She looked at him sadly in the dark.

'So long, kid. Thanks for the nice time.'

She stood on the porch, hearing the sound of his car drive away. There was no music now, and she sensed the dance was over. It must be very late.

When her sister came home soon afterwards, Cora was still standing in the hall, fragmented, vague.

'Oh, hello. What are you doing up so late?'

Cicily was exhilarated; her hair was prettily untidy. Chuck Farnsworth and a fair boy Cora did not know were with her. Escorts. All three were flushed and shiftingly aware of one another. Still immersed in her own experience she understood, yet felt superior.

'Did a car just leave?' asked her sister.

'Yes. It was Len Macintosh.'

'Him!'

'Yes, he wanted Daddy.'

Cicily executed a shudder, and Cora wanted to hit her.

'He probably wanted to sell him some hooch.' Cicily turned to her eager followers. 'Shall we?'

They left together in Chuck's car. Cora knew the routine. It would be scrambled eggs and bacon at the depot. They would wait for the early morning freight train and come home as the sun rose. Let them; let her sister sneer and preen herself. Cora no longer cared. They would never know of her experience tonight. She would never tell anyone. They would not understand, even if she felt like telling them.

In the living room, she collected her poems. Len's glass held a drop of wine. She drank it, thinking about his lips. Upstairs, she put away her poetry and the copy of Keats. With the music silenced, the night seemed to be waiting. Even the crickets were asleep. Her bedside clock said half-past midnight. It would be an hour or so before her parents returned. They were dining up the mountain with a party of friends at the Cooking Club. They'd be late; Cora knew from experience. They and Cicily and Cicily's friends were distant and alien to her thoughts. They did not matter. She wandered into Cicily's room, not bothering to turn on the light. A streetlamp cast a glow, and she saw a single red shoe and discarded clothing. The scent of Cicily's perfume, Jicky, was strong. Cora picked up the atomiser and sprayed herself. Then she unbuttoned her dress—her mother always bought dresses that buttoned up the front, the better, she said, to camouflage Cora's 'puppy fat'.

Cora despised the dress; abruptly she despised her mother because of using the term 'puppy fat'. The unwanted dress fell about her ankles and she stepped out of it. Walking to Cicily's long mirror, she unhooked the fastening of the white cotton bra that bound her abundant breasts like a chaste bandage. Dropping it, she stood for a moment staring at her dim reflection in the mirror. The soft light produced shadows on her body. Cora held her waist and stretched, lifting her breasts. Where was the puppy fat? Her waist looked narrow and her legs were long and straight. Len should see her now. The thought of him made her shiver. She put tentative fingers, the nails bitten short, to her breasts.

Outside in the drive a car door slammed. She dropped her hands. There had been no sound of wheels, or had there? She felt betrayed, spied on. She had barely finished buttoning her dress when she heard her mother coming up the stairs, calling her name.

They met in the hall. Cora hardly heard her mother's solicitous questions, too cheerful by half. Gin. Cora recognised the tone of voice. Murmuring goodnight, she went into her room, closing the door softly, though she would have preferred to bang it. She sat, drooping, on the edge of the bed, emotions roaring. She hated; she loved; she despaired. Then with a shock she remembered her bra, lying still on Cicily's floor. Now she would have to wait until her father and mother had gone to bed, listening for the rumble and chirp of their night voices, before retrieving it. Cicily must not find it and draw inference. Previous excitement drained away; loathing for everything she was not, or felt she never could be, took precedence. When finally she went soft-footed to Cicily's room to pick up the bra, she had made up her mind that soon she would run away. In bed, she lay stiffly, trying to recall Len's face. She could not see it; nor could she think for the moment of a single line of poetry to comfort her. Just before she fell asleep, she told herself that she would not sleep a wink this night or any other.

Stag Line

On the eve of the Great Depression I fell in love. At fourteen one did not equate the two factors. And at fourteen the heart is strong, holding steady to the object of one's affections, in this case a boy three years my senior. He was a scion and we both were products of that slightly absurd stratum of American society, White Anglo-Saxon Protestants—WASPS. I did not understand at that time what a scion was, but heard people refer to him as one—scion, they said, of a large tobacco company. Scriven was his first name and we called him Scrivvy. He came from the East (I was a cattle rancher's daughter from Colorado) and he attended St. Paul's School in Concord, New Hampshire where my eldest brother was also a pupil. After falling in love, my ambition was to attend a school on the Eastern Seaboard, possibly somewhere near Concord.

In view of the Depression and a falling cattle market, this looked improbable. Then help arrived in the form of a rich aunt whose husband was one of those who actually made a profit from the Depression, and who insisted we call her Tante. Vanquishing the bubbles in her champagne glass with a gold swizzle stick, Tante, having quaffed, declared herself prepared to pay my tuition.

The school chosen was Westover in a hamlet called Middlebury in Connecticut and was, of course, for girls only. It was a happy choice because Scrivvy would soon be attending Yale University only a few miles away.

At Westover, which offered a copious helping of the Fine Arts, talk was mostly of boys and marriage. College, Higher Education, were not considerations. After graduating, one had a coming-out party, became a debutante, joined the Junior

League and got married. Pictures of the bride and groom and wedding attendants appeared subsequently in the society pages of *The New York Times*, *The Herald Tribune*, and, of course, regional papers.

I thought of boys too, all the time, Scrivvy somehow incorporating the entire youthful male sex. I thought of them on the hockey field, in classes and chapel, in church while taking communion; during exams and the dreadful cotillions when we had to dance with each other wearing chaste, white muslin uniform dresses and black stockings, these last daringly alternating with a permitted colour called 'gun metal'. The dresses could be covered by flannel capes of various pastel shades. In the daytime, we wore khaki uniforms with brass buttons and wide black patent leather belts fastened by big, brass buckles engraved with the school motto, *Cogitare, Agere, esse*. To Think, To Do, To Be. White linen detachable collars had to be fresh each morning, and pinned to these were black, grosgrain ties. To escape the uniforms, I thought of boys during concerts and during lectures. When Kerensky, the exiled leader of Russia came to speak to us, my attention wandered because not only did he use his native language, but he was neither young nor good-looking. The interpreter seemed better, though not overwhelming.

Later, in class, we were told of a person called Trotsky who was some sort of bad guy. He made small impression on me. Inadvertently, for some odd reason, unknown, therefore undisputed, our school song 'Raise Now to Westover' was sung to the tune of the White Russian anthem. Paradoxically, the large room where Kerensky lectured was named Red Hall. This had less to do with politics than with the lush red carpet that covered the hall and climbed the double staircase.

It would seem that world politics and the state of mankind failed to move us. Yet, the human brain cells being wonderfully arranged, something must have remained: a mention of Trotsky, (who was he?), Revolution and the word Bolshie. Mostly, however, at that stage, we were bereft of social conscience. We were gilded, even copper-plated youth. The copper came from the Guggenheim smelters in Colorado, and the winds passing above them grew tainted. Yet no Guggenheim daughter graced Red Hall, or wrestled with the Honour System by which the school was run. We were overfed, white Anglo-Saxons, and stupefyingly Christian.

By my third year, Scrivvy the scion was well-installed at Yale. My hopes stayed strong, but since he did not write or come to see me, I could only prepare for vague eventuality by learning to Charleston from the Negro maids, trying to diet and conforming to accepted standards of behaviour.

The cotillions continued. One Saturday a month we were permitted to entertain boys, recruited usually from neighbouring prep schools such as Choate or Taft. Some of these may have been scions but only one singled me out for attention, even though I wore glasses. He was a 'greasy grind', another 'Four Eyes'. We stumped around the dance floor to thumping rhythms from an upright piano played by our music teacher, Miss Wolfe. I knew a greasy grind to be admirable in his way, intellectual, one who studied. But I would never have admitted this; to do so would have destroyed my efforts to conform.

Near the end of term that third year, with spring softening the New England air, an incident occurred to change the course of my thinking. It happened on a Sunday evening during what was called 'quiet hour'. Four or five of us were gathered illegally in a room at the front of the school overlooking the road through Middlebury and the village green, on the far side of which was the white clapboard church we attended on Sundays. The meeting was illicit on two counts. We were forbidden to leave our rooms during quiet hour, and in so doing we violated the Honour System.

I was excited, having never before been invited. Two senior girls added glamour and I listened as they spoke of coming débuts and subsequent marriage as though both were inevitable. That they were did not disturb me. I hoped then my own future would be similar.

That was at 6:00 in the evening. By 8:00 p.m. my viewpoint and with it my destiny had changed.

The reason for the gathering was simple: boys, or rather 'men', Yale men. They came in their cars and parked outside the school. Feigning punctures, they changed tyres frequently, then lingered, calling to their girls of the moment who flung wide the windows to lean out. Flippancy and flirtation filled the air, never more so as when Mary Ellen, the prettiest senior, held court. She had numbers of admirers, but graciously distributed them among her friends if the man of her choice turned up.

I stood back from the window, hopeful but not really expecting anything. Then a girl at the window turned to say someone was calling my name.

Inconceivable! But Scrivvy the scion was indeed out there. I could not see him in the dusk, but heard him call. His tones were not those of tender assignation. They were jocular and even sarcastic. He was acting for the benefit of the other girls. I felt bereft, and could not speak.

Below someone blew his car horn. Then a light came on. I guessed it to be one of those large, nickle-plated searchlights, as popular a concomitant on current automobiles as a cut-out. It flashed, radiated slowly and came to rest on my expectant, embarrassed face.

'Hey, Four Eyes! You're in the limelight for the first and last time.'

It was the scion. I pretended laughter and as the light went out, so did I, all hope fractured, spirits quenched. No one spoke as I left the room.

The wound was deep, and from it protest had been born. After that, I ceased to conform. I studied hard and became a greasy grind. My thoughts turned to Higher Education on long, solitary walks. I read philosophy and learned about socialism. Yet still I hesitated. The humiliating experience of Scrivvy had not been enough to eliminate dreams of boys. I dwelt halfway between expectancy and a vague vindictiveness, uncomfortably perched on a dividing line at equal distance from Trotsky on the one hand and hedonism on the other.

In my senior year I applied myself to the role of intellectual. The proletariat ceased to be 'out there' and I wished to identify with them. I edited the school magazine and wrote poetry.

Graduation came at last. I went to visit Tante in California where I told her I would never become a debutante or join the Junior League. Tante was forbearing and gave me money for a trip to New York to 'think things over'. I felt there was nothing to think about, but took the train anyway.

In Grand Central Station, carrying my fitted green crocodile-skin suitcase, a gift from Tante, I walked up the long ramp, through the great cathedral hall and out to a city effervescent with autumnal light and air: sparkle and bubble, New York in 1929, New York before the Wall Street Crash; the imminent Crash. Possibly men were already standing grey-faced, in queues. Possibly others were hawking apples along the strident excitement of Lexington Avenue where I walked, but I did not notice. Vanity had made me remove my glasses.

In the Biltmore Hotel, I sat on a low couch with Alvina, a school friend whom I had not seen since graduation. Tea was served and we drank and ate and heard the music issuing from a room nearby. Alvina said it was for the *thé dansant*, a feature of the Biltmore. The music distracted me and I did not listen too carefully to what Alvina was saying. Then a word penetrated: anthropology.

'I'm majoring in it,' she said.

I knew she was the only one of our class who had transgressed. She had enrolled in Smith College. I was impressed, hearing about the anthropology, imagining ivy-covered walls, elms stirring with birds, students arm in arm or carrying books.

The music compelled. 'You're the cream in my coffee...'

Alvina, a kind-hearted girl, understood my mind was not on her talk of classes and schedules and ultimate diplomas. She asked me if I were going to a class-mate's coming-out party that same night. Here it was, then, demanding courage and conviction. Trotsky versus Irving Berlin.

I said I had nothing to wear. Alvina said she would lend me something, and that we could telephone Faith, the hostess, when we got back to the brownstone in the Seventies where I was staying with Alvina and her parents.

The decision seemed to have been made for me. I agreed to go. After all, it wasn't *my* coming-out party.

The borrowed dress belonged to Alvina's sister, who was abroad. It was backless and sleeveless and of pink, *moiré* silk. The wrap-around skirt fell to just below my knees, each layer fringed like a Spanish shawl. It fitted me rather well; then, a black velvet cape, borrowed from Alvina's mother, an evening bag glistening with sequins, flesh-coloured stockings rolled at the knees, and black, strapped, satin shoes. I was ready for a sortie into alien territory. Better to think of the evening as a trivial beginning to my adventures in a world where there was no honour system.

The party was held at Sherry's, an elegant restaurant on Fifth Avenue almost directly opposite the Plaza Hotel. Flaming Youth had only recently been doused, but the smoke of their departure still hung about.

I followed Alvina into Sherry's feeling worse than if I had been going to a school cotillion with nothing but a greasy grind in view. The foyer was crowded with young men in tuxedos. They watched us and uttered knowing remarks which we could not hear. Alvina walked serenely past them. Moving nervously in her wake, I heard a familar voice.

'Not you!'

It was the scion, all black and white, his hair shining with pomade. We stared at each other. He could not call me Four Eyes because I was not wearing my glasses.

'Hello, Scrivvy.'

His surprise at seeing me in this giddy ambiance gave me confidence. I greeted Faith, left my cape in the Ladies' Room across a glittering dancefloor, and obediently followed an usher to a table, one of dozens, each seating six people. Flowers scented the air. They were set about the room in huge vases, quivered in corsages on the bosoms of girls, brightened the tables. As my nervousness returned, I stared at a bowl of mixed blooms and wondered unpleasantly which hospital on the morrow would benefit from all this extravagant beauty.

I was alone at the table with two strange couples and an empty chair.

Food was eventually served; I could not eat. The happy chatter of the others emphasised my plight. I wished fervently to be a thousand miles away.

Then there was music. People got up to dance. I took a sip of fruit cup, feeling again most dreadfully in the limelight, as obvious a wallflower, as though a sash across my chest announced the fact. I squeezed a roll, rigid with misery, and patted my bobbed hair.

Reprieve came at last in the person of a cheerful young man who introduced himself as Harley. Faith, he said, had sent him. Faith indeed. I accepted his invitation to dance. The music, of course, was pre-swing. The band was Meyer Davis, wonderfully brassy and growling. The music excited my feet. Harley spoke of the band; I spoke of the floor. The music was swell; the floor was smooth. Then I noticed them.

Crowded together in the middle of the dancefloor were the stags, the extra young men invited to make the evening more exciting or, and this was the deadly aspect, to rescue males from being 'stuck' with the girls they partnered. I had heard of stags. They were a malignant social innovation breeding neurosis and insecurity. It was never the other way round. That the boy who was 'stuck' could be a clumsy dancer with unpleasant breath did not occur to the male orientated period of the Twenties. The stag line milled and watched, grinned and whispered to each other. They might have been pawing the ground. I feared them.

As we circled, I noticed a boy dancing near us was holding something out behind his partner's back. I was too short-sighted to identify the object, but guessed it to be a dollar bill. I had

heard rumours of this kind of bribery at school. The boy wanted
to be rid of his partner. Presently he was recovering himself
among his fellow stags. I imagined how the girl must feel and
wondered uneasily if this was to be my fate.

During the second trip to the dancefloor, a boy cut in and I
did the Charleston with him, finding my lessons from the maids
at Westover to have been well-taken. When a second boy
appeared, I knew joyfully that no dollar bill had exchanged
hands. Success intoxicated me. I kicked up my heels like a good
dancing daughter.

'I'm sitting on top of the world,' sang one of the musicians
appropriately.

We Charlestoned once more and tried the Black Bottom. The
music was loud and beautiful. Boys kept cutting in. I felt like
a red hot momma.

With a silken swish my dress fell down. The hooks and eyes
fastening the waist had parted and the skirt unwound until its
fringe draped my ankles. No one really noticed except my
partner, and some of the stags, as I pulled up my dress and
walked casually as I could to the Ladies' Room. A maid in a
black dress and white apron fastened me up, but said sceptically
she did not think the hooks would hold.

She was right. While we were executing a fast foxtrot, the
dress fell again. This time the maid resorted to a large safety
pin. It held. By now I had become someone to be noticed, to
be cut in on. I found myself changing partners so quickly there
was no time to finish a sentence. Somewhere in the wild mosaic
of the evening, I felt certain the scion's face would appear,
though I did not think much about it because other faces
were looking admiringly into mine. Other lips spoke kindly or
suggestive words, and my excitement was such that when
Scrivvy cut in, I could only look at him and laugh.

'You've made a spectacle of yourself,' he said.

At one time, his disagreeable tone would have destroyed my
self-esteem. Not tonight. He seemed merely ridiculous. How
could I ever have yearned for that narrow face and the black

eyes that were too close to his nose? But he was tall and strong and, surprisingly, held me rather too tightly. The band played the Varsity Drag.

'Why're you laughing?'

'I'm having a wonderful time, Scrivvy. It's a nifty party.'

I wanted to tell him I was in the limelight in a happy way, was loving every exhibitionistic moment. Someone else cut in just then and the conversation stopped.

The party finally came to an end. Where was Alvina? She had waved to me hours ago and then I'd forgotten her.

'Take you home?'

It was the scion. My moment of triumph seemed less important than it might have been even a short time ago. I knew Scrivvy was mine now, if I wanted him.

It was nearly dawn when we emerged from Sherry's. The trees in Central Park were outlined against a brightening sky. We walked back to Alvina's house. All the way, I flirted with Scrivvy, discovering in myself the possibilities of a desired girl who knew her immediate power to refuse. The excitement of the party sustained me, but I felt it would be the last of its kind. More than ever I did not wish to conform. Nor, it seemed a few minutes later, did sexual play assume importance, at least not from Scrivvy. At Alvina's door, he asked me to invite him in. I said it was too late.

'Oh, come on.'

It was almost a whine. When I shook my head, he grabbed me and misdirected wet kisses about my face. I pulled free.

'Goodbye, Scrivvy. I'll be seeing you.'

I shut the door in his face. The beeswax silence of the hall was admonishment. The spotlight had been turned off. In my room, I sat on the bed too excited to sleep. The evening flashed by in giddy retrospect. I unpinned the fateful *moiré* dress, hanging it in the closet. So long, dress. So long, many things.

Two days later, I walked down the ramp of Grand Central Station to the lower level where trains waited impatiently to be on their way. The steps were out; redcaps toted luggage;

porters waited to cry 'All aboard!' As I walked along looking
for my Pullman, a man smiled at me. I smiled back.

That evening, waiting in the club car for my berth to be
made up, I saw him again. He was florid, handsome and dressed
in a way I recognised to be vulgar, but I rather liked it. He sat
down beside me.

'Mind?' He bent closer. 'Say, you're cute as a bug's ear.
Going far?'

'Yes. All the way to California.'

'Well, now. Going to be in pictures?'

'I'm going to college.'

It was sad. He appeared to lose interest. From being a bug's
ear, I had sunk to being a greasy grind. He concentrated on
opening a package of Lucky Strike cigarettes. Lighting up, he
looked with pleasure through a cloud of smoke at a girl who
had entered the club car. She wore a blue bow in her blonde
curls and there were similar bows on her square-toed shoes. She
walked with a bounce and I thought her to be much more a
bug's ear type than I. My companion stared. Suddenly I was
reminded of a dollar bill, hopefully waved. I stood up.

'Going already?'

I knew he was pleased. Perhaps he would manoeuvre the girl
into my vacant chair. I said goodnight and walked through the
swaying train. The whistle mourned and a huge apprehension
seized me. It was done, and there could be no retreat because
that would be craven, like accepting the stag line and self-
abasement. I must study, must widen my horizons and change
the concept of a greasy grind. I thought back to New York. In
the context of my new and enlightened decision, it would have
been good to say I had seen a man selling apples on a street
corner and that I had bought one, two, three from him. But it
would have been a lie.

Before the Godfather

The Upper East side of Manhattan, around Yorkville, is a mixture of extreme wealth and borderline poverty where the small tradesman fights inflation and taxes with the frantic single-mindedness of a New Yorker in travail. It was thus in 1962 when I moved there; it is much the same today. White bastions of new apartment houses fraught with balconies have arisen; bars and restaurants have changed hands; a laundromat has ceased to exist; the kaleidoscope of a neighbourhood has shifted slightly. But 82nd Street teems; the oompah Deutschland atmosphere prevails; German is still spoken in the stores where German food is sold; and on street corners the Nazi *Bund* still holds meetings.

In 1962 the summer nights were as tropical as they are today, possibly cleaner, but sailors in their whites walked 82nd Street looking for girls and fun, and it might have been anywhere in the Far East. I envied the sailors. They did not have to be lonely, nor were they afraid. I knew both loneliness and fear but could not bring myself to enter one of the 'swinging singles' clubs, being both the wrong age and too alien. So I searched for a bar and restaurant where I might go each evening after work, where I would be accepted and could possibly make friends; in short, a local.

For a lone woman in those days and in that special neighbourhood, fear had been augmented by the recent double murder of two girls in an apartment house a couple of blocks above where I lived over an upholstery store on York Avenue. It had been a particularly squalid crime, and was as yet unsolved. Juxtaposition to this kind of death made one distinctly nervous, but it would be better to be nervous among friends than at

home alone. I began to search. Between 78th and 79th on Third
Avenue I found a neat looking restaurant called Bon Appetite.
The spelling was inconclusive. French? Italian? Both, Amer-
icanised? I decided to try it.

The bar was a semi-circle; the stools upholstered. To the
right of the door was a solid-looking table surrounded by chairs,
but no one was there. The restaurant proper lay beyond the
bar and it was pleasant to see white table-cloths. A couple of
waitresses moved among the tables, and there was a merry clink
of cutlery and glasses. The air smelled deliciously of Italian
food.

I advanced, nodding to the bartender, who had looked up
as the door opened. He was youngish with dark hair worn
unfashionably short and smooth. His suit was surprisingly conventional.

'Want a table?'

The waitress was about forty with a sumptuous pile of glistening, pinky hair. It was a shade I had never seen before, and
the entire edifice had been lacquered almost for posterity. The
face beneath was pretty in an Irish kind of way. Her make-up
was admirable. I was to learn her name was Lucille and that
she was the chief waitress. The second waitress was auxiliary,
and varied from week to week.

Lucille seated me and suggested spaghetti with clam sauce.
I accepted her judgement, ordering a glass of white wine to go
with the clams. Next time, I would stop at the bar for an
aperitif.

The clientèle was mixed. A young party of four were drinking
hard and laughing. Three tables were occupied by lone diners
like myself, a woman and two men. At a table deep in the room
next to the kitchen doors sat a policeman. His cap lay on the
table beside his plate and he appeared to be an expert with
spaghetti. My own arrived, and accompanying it was a stocky
man in his fifties with a large, handsome head. His hair was
grey and thick; he resembled a Roman emperor in a soiled,
white apron.

'Welcome,' he said. 'I'm Mike Penterelli. You enjoying your clams?'

He pulled out the extra chair and sat down. The waitress hovered. Mike smiled at her.

'Bring a carafe of white, doll. On the house,' he added.

He watched me eat, studying each mouthful and nodding his head in satisfaction 'Good, eh? Good. You won't get clam sauce like that anywhere else in Manhattan.'

When the wine arrived I asked him to share it with me. 'Not me. Lucille, bring me a Chivas on the rocks.'

We drank. After a time half the carafe had gone. All the while Mike talked or asked me questions and listened to me talking. I found it easy to tell him about myself, my divorce, my children. He thought it tough I had to be separated from them.

'But I guess you need the money.'

Clients came and went, greeting Mike who in turn said, 'Howza boy, Gerry?' or 'Say, Ruth, you're more beautiful every day.'

The policeman finished his meal and departed with a laconic, 'See ya, Mike.'

'Neighbourhood cop,' said Mike. 'I do him a turn, he does me one. Besides, he likes spaghetti.'

When I left, Mike escorted me to the door, pausing to introduce me to the bartender who, close up, looked like Gene Kelly when young. He nodded, putting a hand to his mouth and smiling around it. Later I discovered a front tooth was missing. His name was Russell Cushing. Mike called him Russ.

'He's got savvy, y'know. Joe College.'

Russ looked embarrassed. He touched the knot of his tie.

'This young lady won't know what that antiquated expression means.'

Mike looked delighted. 'Whad did I tell you? He's got savvy.'

I said I had heard the expression before and asked Russ where he had gone to college.

'Oh, just a little backwater place in New Hampshire.'

He appeared reluctant to talk about it. I said I hoped I would see him again; Russ ducked his head politely and Mike walked me to the door.

'Sure you'll be back,' he said. 'We like you. It's good for you to have a regular place.'

He opened the door for me and stood for a moment on the threshold as I started to walk away.

'Hey, like to ask you something before you go.'

'Of course.'

'Did you like Franklin D. Roosevelt?'

I was pleased to say 'yes', that I had in fact voted for Roosevelt—my first time—in his last term.

'I knew it. Can always tell. You're one of us.'

This made me uneasy. Later I would wonder sometimes what would have happened to our friendship had I disliked Roosevelt, soon realising how pointless was the hypothesis. Mike's ambiance would not have attracted a Roosevelt hater. Oddly, he seemed indifferent to President Kennedy. As time passed it seemed less strange. Mike was rooted in the Thirties, in the Depression, looking on Roosevelt as his saviour. Then came the war and the day of Roosevelt's death when the nation came to a stop. Mike's passion was as strong as his opposites who so hated Roosevelt that when he did die, they threw parties and sang their kind of bigoted hallelujahs.

It became my habit to take an evening meal at Mike's. The food was ample and beautifully cooked by Mike. Very soon I had my own special stool at the bar.

'Two brains,' Mike remarked seeing me in conversation with Russell. 'You should get along good.'

I was touched that to Mike my job as a minor editor could be equated with extensive intellect. Yet conversation with Russ was enjoyable. Mike was right. We did get along. Gradually, Russ revealed a wide knowledge of books, though continued to be reticent about himself. He had only attended college for one term, but this was enough for Mike who remained unshakeable in his conviction that Russ qualified for a PhD with the best of them.

As time passed, I began to wonder about Mike's family. He had a wife, Russ told me, and a teenage son who sometimes helped in the kitchen. But Mrs. Penterelli never came to the restaurant. It would not be fitting, Russ told me, according to Mike's way of life. On the other hand, his sister Rosie helped out in the kitchen.

'A case of arrested development,' Russ said. 'Strictly out to lunch. Poor Rosie.'

When I got to know Rosie better, I understood how apt was this euphemism. Rosie was never there, though she made sounds and gestures to indicate her presence. But the words she uttered seldom bore much relationship to what was being discussed; she would say 'mornin'' even while her eyes bypassed one's face, searching for nebulous horizons and shadowy shapes. 'Yeah, yeah,' she would say eagerly, entering the conversation obliquely, speaking parrot-fashion and looking anxiously towards her beloved brother for reassurance.

Mike adored her. He watched over her and would let no one come near with observations even hinting at ridicule. In return, she gave him her devotion and, a husky young woman, scrubbed and swept and sang loudly. She had a lot of curly black hair and there must have been a time in her extreme youth when she had been beautiful. Sometimes she came to hang around the bar and Russ, seeing her coming would groan, 'Oh, God'.

Rosie was in love with Russ. But it was a fickle love. She offered her affections and her Rubens body to all and sundry if they happened to catch her fancy. But there was always Mike to intervene between his sister and anyone who considered taking advantage of the offer. Rosie was safe for the time being. Though she and Mike were American, they had been born in Sicily, their parents emigrating to the United States when the children were small. I learned this from Russ. I also learned that Mike had rescued Russ when he found the bartender lying drunk in a doorway before the cops came along. It was a familiar road, Russ told me: Irish bars, the Bowry, the Salvation Army, the law. As he spoke, a hand went up to cover the gap in his teeth.

I had by now become friendly with the regular customers, but had not yet seen anyone sitting at the big table by the door. When I asked Russ why this was so, he retreated into ambiguity, murmuring something about 'Mike's friends'.

Then one night there appeared a group of men, stiff in their dark suits, all around Mike's age, save for one, a tall, handsome man in his seventies with abundant white hair and a lofty bearing. They seated themselves at the table, the big man at the head. Russ saw me looking and as he served me a drink said under his breath, 'The Family'.

Before I could ask more, he was busy taking orders for drinks. I stayed quietly on my stool, watching, then realised someone was watching me. I turned my head to see a young man in an electric blue suit staring with strange eyes. His pupils were huge, giving him an unfocused look.

'How about introducing me, Russ?'

So it was I met Eddie who, it transpired, was the big, white-haired man's chauffeur. The car he drove was a long, sand-coloured Cadillac sparkling with chromium trim. Whenever the Family arrived, the No Parking sign outside Bon Appetite mysteriously disappeared. The resident policeman never said a word. There was an understanding.

From time to time, Mike's enthusiasm for the late Roosevelt would manifest itself in a need for 'a little old party'. When this mood overtook him, he would lock the doors after having turned out those he considered to be Roosevelt-haters. I marvelled at his presumption. People left angrily, but most of them returned in time. Perhaps it was the food.

If the Family were present, they too would join in. Drinks flowed, but I noticed the chauffeur with the electric blue suit never took more than Coca-Cola. He could not afford to drink, Russ told me. He needed the money for his habit. A junkie! My first. It was a long way from de Quincey, I thought, who would never in any case have worked for the Mafia, as I was now beginning to understand they were.

Mike never talked about Sicily. As far as he was concerned, he was American. Anything to do with true-blue US ethics interested him, yet there was always a New York cynicism in what he said. He knew how hard he had worked to be successful, and no one could take that away from him. At the same time, he was generous, lending money to those who needed it, like Jim Eckhardt, a printer who came regularly to the Bon Appetite and who wanted new equipment for his business. He cared for Russ; he protected Rosie; he advised Lucille and paid her extra salary when her husband left her; he made certain no random drinker bothered me. He was funny and crude and kind. We all loved him.

It was his kindness that allowed me to introduce him to Milly Stanhope, or vice versa. Milly was out of place in the essentially conventional ambiance of the Bon Appetite but I felt sorry for her. She was 18, a flower child, friend of young friends. She always needed money or a pad where she could crash. She carried a guitar on her slender back and seemed always to be breathless, though it could have been indigestion. She ate junk food because she was poor. From time to time I fed her, and perhaps it was her enthusiasm when putting away a plate of his spaghetti that finally decided Mike. He agreed to pay her $25 for an evening's entertainment, with a free meal thrown in.

Milly opened on a Saturday when the restaurant was full. Even the Family table was complete. Milly, her long, straight blonde hair washed—and ironed, as was the fad of the day— perched herself on a bar stool, guitar at the ready, while the clientèle stared and grinned. Mike came out of his kitchen, minus his apron and wearing a pale-blue linen jacket and grey trousers. He looked thoughtfully at Milly in her trailing skirt and peasant blouse. When she flipped the skirt to make herself comfortable I noticed unhappily that her feet were bare and filthy.

'This is a song,' she began, and suddenly looked terrified.

'Don't be scared, kid,' said Mike with a kind smile.

Milly played a chord or two and began in a thin, little voice to sing 'Blowing in the Wind', a song recorded by Peter, Paul and Mary but not one, I thought, glancing around, which had been heard by more than a handful in the room. When she had finished there was a clap or two and a feeling of imminent departure. But they waited as Mike nodded to her to continue.

This time she announced 'We Shall Overcome' and there was an uneasy murmur when she further explained that it was a Civil Rights song. The words 'Commy', 'Pinko' and 'bleeding heart' seemed to me in my concern for Milly to dance about the bar. I looked at Mike, wondering when, in his life of devotion to the US and Roosevelt, Frank Sinatra had taken over from Woody Guthrie if, in truth, he had ever heard of the latter.

'Oh, deep in my heart,' sang Milly, 'I do believe/That we shall overcome some day.'

Only Mike, Jim Eckhardt, Russ and I clapped. A voice from the Family table said 'Strictly from hunger', and Mike frowned.

'Give us another, doll,' he said.

This time Milly launched into 'House of the Rising Sun' and Mike, faintly recognising something resembling jazz, tried to beat time. It did not work. People were talking now against the singing and the final lines, 'And it's been the ruin of many a poor girl/And me, oh God, for one', were lost.

Against the rising volume of background talk, Milly tried bravely to give them 'What Have They Done with the Rain'. Useless. She put down her guitar.

'I don't think,' she began.

'How about "Danny Boy"?' asked someone.

Milly said she didn't know it. Someone else asked for 'Stardust', another for 'Old Man River'. She looked confused.

'Oh, she don't know songs like that,' Mike said. 'You're just showing your age. This girl's a hippy and anybody who don't know what that is don't know shit from Shinola. Now give her a hand.'

Amid tepid applause, he thanked Milly, saying she'd 'done great, real great', handing her $25 from the till. He walked her towards the door, his arm around her shoulders. Just before letting her out, he gave the shoulders a little squeeze and said something I could not hear. Then he closed and locked the door, turning to the assembled guests.

'Now,' he said, rubbing his hands. 'We'll have us a little old party. I feel like celebrating.'

The curtains were drawn, drinks were on the house, and soon Dean Martin's baritone cancelled out any lingering vibrations from Pete Seeger. In the ensuing hubbub Mike told me how sorry he was to turn Milly down.

'The clientèle don't go for that stuff.'

But he seemed genuinely upset and this fact, plus his general kindness, made me agree to accept an invitation, extended through Mike, to spend an evening with Cheech, the big man from the Family table. Mike seemed eager for me to go.

I was uneasy, but kept telling myself it was an adventure. To my surprise, Eddie of the electric blue suit and the drowned eyes did not drive. Cheech took the wheel and I sat beside him. It was around 10:00 at night, and we drove up into an unfamiliar part of Manhattan. I lost track of the streets, only guessing that we were somewhere on the upper-upper East side. There were few lighted shops, and few people in the streets. Where there was street lighting, it showed boarded-up houses, black alleys, abandonment. We stopped in front of one of the blank buildings from which no gleam of light showed.

'This'll interest you,' said Cheech who had spoken little during the drive, apart from mentioning a restaurant he planned to open soon in midtown.

We walked up to the door across which a board appeared to have been nailed. Cheech rapped sharply, and to my astonishment a small, concealed grill opened and a voice asked us to identify ourselves.

'Cheech.'

The door opened immediately. Inside was a pefectly fitted

bar with red leather seats. Men in dark suits and ties nodded to Cheech who led me to the back of the bar and through a door guarded by a young man who stepped aside to let us through.

The scene within was astonishing. Here the floors above had been removed and the room rose up to the roof giving a cathedral-like effect. Shadows and cigarette smoke shrouded the corners. There were fifty or more men in the room, all standing around gaming tables and machines I did not recognise.

'What are they doing?'

'Roulette and one-armed bandits,' Cheech told me.

No one looked at us. I only partially understood what I was seeing. Playing one-armed bandits was a racket; it was illegal. I followed Cheech back into the bar, feeling uncomfortable. It was the closest I had been to this kind of organised crime. I wanted no part of it.

Drinks were waiting on a table when we returned to the bar. The door between the rooms must have been reinforced because here the sound of men's voices, murmuring, shouting, cursing, the click of the machines and of dice, could not be heard. Here there were low-voiced conversations and a jukebox in one corner played cocktail-type music, giving off rainbow gleams. We did not stay long, and I was relieved. Cheech dropped me at my door, saying nothing about seeing me again, which was the way I wanted it.

Soon after this curious episode, Mike announced that he intended selling the Bon Appetite and buying a new place. This conversation took place late one night. Only Russ and I were present.

'What do you want to change for, Mike? You're doing all right here.' Russ sounded worried.

Mike was impatient. No, no, he wanted a different kind of place, something with class.

'I dig those red jackets.'

Later Russ and I talked about it. Russ was worried.

'I think he's competing with Cheech.' I asked what was wrong with this, to which Russ replied 'Cheech has muscle. Mike could get in his way.'

It was late on a Saturday morning when my telephone rang. Lucille sounded hysterical. Had I seen the *Daily News*? She did not wait for my answer.

'It's Mike. He's been shot.'

I rushed out to buy the paper. It was all there on the front page—a spread with a photograph of Mike lying back in the front seat of his car behind the wheel, dead, shot through the heart, the paper said. The police, it went on, were calling it a gangland murder.

The bar would be open; Russ might know more, and I felt the need of a friend. Walking along, I thought the bewildered thoughts of one who has never before been touched by violent and deliberate death.

Russ had an open copy of the *Daily News* on the bar and as I came in said despairingly: 'I told him not to do it.'

'But what did he do?'

'You know those big ideas he had about a new restaurant? Well, he decided to put some into operation. He cashed a cheque and went off to pick up some cases of J & B Whisky. Class stuff, he called it.'

He kept polishing a glass he held, rubbing it needlessly. 'They didn't take the money. It was on the seat beside him, in cash.'

'Yes, I read about it.'

'Seven thousand dollars,' said Russ.

We were silent for a moment. It was hard to visualise how many cases of whisky that much money could buy.

'The police will never find out who did it,' Russ went on. 'They won't even try, not when it's a gangland murder.'

The day of the funeral, Russ and Lucille and I took a taxi to the mortuary where Mike was lying in state. It was a gloomy building with two big rooms opening out from a hall. The place was crowded. Men wore black mourning bands; the women were all dressed in black and seemed to have had their hair freshly done. Never having met Mike's wife, I could not pick her out from the other women, but Rosie was there, sitting near the front door, sobbing and swaying. Unlike the rest, her dress was brightly coloured with a floral pattern; her hair was wild.

In the first room a receiving line awaited the mourners, and Russ introduced me to Mike's wife who was pretty and fat, with sad, black eyes. She pressed my hand against her black satin bosom, the histrionic little gesture bringing tears to my eyes.

'You are a friend; any friendsa Mike issa my friend.'

A queue had formed outside the room containing Mike's coffin. When it came to my turn I looked first at his hands around which had been entwined a rosary. This seemed out of character. Yet, had I ever known his private beliefs, apart from his love of Roosevelt? He was dressed in a smart grey suit and blue shirt and tie which, had they been open, would have matched his eyes. His thick grey hair was beautifully combed; he looked relaxed and quite lifelike. I sent him some goodbye thoughts, then, lifting my head, met Cheech's eyes across the open coffin. He too wore a mourning band and was smiling sorrowfully. Then in the hall behind me Rosie shrieked:

'Mike told me to wait. I waited and I waited and he didn't come. Now he never will.'

One of the mourners, a handsome young man with curly hair, crossed her line of vision and her weeping stopped abruptly.

'Hiya, Angelo,' she called in a normal voice. 'Long time no see.'

But immediately afterwards, she returned to weeping.

'Let's get out of here,' Russ said behind me.

It was what I wanted; so did Lucille.

We found a taxi.

'I guess we all know where we're going.'

At the Bon Appetite, Russ unlocked the door and we settled at the bar, large drinks in hand. The discussion began slowly. All of us were aware that the time for jocular reference in this place might not return, ever. Mike had died by violence; and there was no room for gentle sorrow. Talk moved to the near future. What would happen to the restaurant?

Russ smiled cynically. 'Cheech,' he said. 'He already bought it. That's where Mike got the money for a new place.'

Cheech! I thought of him at the funeral and knew suddenly with an awful kind of certainty who had killed Mike, directly or indirectly.

'You staying on?' Lucille asked Russ.

Russ was watching me watching my horrid conclusion. Catching my eye, he shook his head with a kind of warning. Then he put his hand to his mouth in the familiar, defensive gesture.

'For a while,' he told Lucille, and looked away.

I finished my drink and said goodnight. A sense of loss made the bar oppressive. Lucille leaned forward on her stool to pat my shoulder.

'So long, honey.'

A few days later, I went back but the door to the Bon Appetite was padlocked. A New York episode had come to an end. I did not forget Mike altogether; he had been too vivid, too kind, and the nature of his death sharpened my memory, especially a few months later when John F. Kennedy also died by the gun.

About that horrendous time I bumped into Milly who had dropped out of sight after her abortive evening of song. She looked better than when I had last seen her and this was soon explained when she told me she had gone home for a while. Good food and rest prepared her for a new onslaught on Manhattan. We spoke, of course, of Kennedy's assassination. I said it reminded me of Mike and she asked me why. When I told her, she was appalled, never having seen the paper or been back to the restaurant.

'That's really, really awful,' she said.

Then she told me that when she left that night, Mike had given her another $20, saying how badly he felt at turning her away.

We were silent for a moment, remembering the evening; remembering Mike.

'He said I should go home,' Milly said after a moment. 'And he told me to go on singing.'

She shifted her guitar case, preparing to leave me.

'He was cool,' she said.

All the Little Wars

Memory is usually selective, but it does have a disconcerting way of arriving unbidden. Piano music heard around twilight always brings back to me old—he seemed old—Mr. Rosenzweig, the German Jewish refugee who had been billeted in a house next to the one I shared with my youngest brother (not yet drafted) in Los Angeles during the Second World War.

Mr. Rosenzweig had a long, despairing face and tended to scurry as though anticipating the hour of curfew to which he and other refugees were subjected. He was testy, suspicious and, with justification, leaned to violence. This violence showed itself when he mistook the Red Indian swastika on my brother's belt buckle to be the more sinister Nazi symbol. I don't know if he ever really understood the difference, though we tried to explain that the arms of the Indian symbol were turned in a different direction from Hitler's emblem. Whatever, he appeared to forgive us and offered to give me piano lessons. But by then I had been drawn into the war effort.

We Americans came tardily to the carnage but we came with enthusiasm. Pain arrived later. But first there were blockbusters, Churchill's speeches, for which one arose at 4.00 a.m., Roosevelt's Fireside Chats and Bundles for Britain. There was also 'Mrs. Miniver' with Greer Garson and Walter Pidgeon. We pretended to find it sentimental, but secretly loved it.

After Pearl Harbor we felt we were honest participants, sympathising with the man across the street from us who emerged that Sunday of December 7, 1941 in his pyjamas and dressing gown, standing on his neat lawn and staring skywards. But not a Japanese plane was to be seen. No bombs fell then or ever on American soil. What happened to our Blitz? A few days later a Japanese submarine did fire on an oil refinery up the coast road to Santa Barbara, and there were rumours of enemy aircraft so intense that the Army brought their anti-aircraft guns into play. The result of this was to tie up traffic with an ensuing loss of man hours and much wasted ammunition.

But the Government felt inspired to round up all the Japanese in the city. Gardeners, houseboys, teachers, shopkeepers, students, lawyers and doctors vanished overnight. The flower shop near our house from which lute music sounded in the evenings was closed and silent. Anyone at all with Japanese blood—never mind being American born—was hustled off to concentration camps. At the time we thought it an unfortunate necessity.

What could a young woman of little experience do in those patriotic days, short of joining the Armed Services? Luckily I heard the Northrop Aircraft Company on the outskirts of Los Angeles, in a suburb called Hawthorne, was hiring women for the first time in its history. I applied and was taken on as a file clerk in the tool division. The job, involving heavy wooden file cabinets was not made easier by active male chauvinism, usually extended in wisecracks filled with sexual innuendo, or the remark 'Women!' spat out contemptuously as the speaker walked by.

But it seemed important to persevere. I shared a car pool and, working the early shift, marched from the parking lot in the dark, carrying a lunch pail with a sentimental feeling of togetherness.

This did not last long, dispelled by general cynicism which caused draughtsmen to draw slant-eyed little men, obviously the enemy, on blueprints which were processed and enlarged before the culprit could be caught. It was a manifestation of behind-the-lines fatigue. Boredom. We were shut into this blacked-out building 'for the duration'.

A crude kind of sexuality prevailed, making it difficult for the female minority of two. Tool machine parts were brought to our notice: tits, rachet drills, bastard files, female gauges, pricks, punches, counter bores and, of course, cocks. But as time passed one learned indifference which spiked the guns of the opposition in this, yet another, conflict.

Yet we all felt a pride when Northrop's secret night fighter, the P-61, or as it had been dubbed, the Black Widow, was finished and we were allowed to watch the first flight, thereby losing valuable hours of work. It was a wicked looking craft, black as its name with strange wings suggesting those ultimately developed in one of Northrop's most brilliant inventions, the Flying Wing.

Air-borne early one morning amid cheers, the fighter vanished. An hour later, back at our toil, we heard it had crashed in the Arizona Desert. 'Too much tail for one man to handle,' workers said coarsely. It was a typical male aircraft worker's joke, adding ammunition to the sexual struggle.

By now both this and the heavy wooden file cabinets were becoming tedious. Machine tools with all their importance held no interest. I made up my mind to leave, using illness as an excuse to take a day off and look for another job.

The Douglas Aircraft Company at Santa Monica was my next employer. Pointing out that I was 'not the type' for assembly line work (by their standards) they put me through many tests, physical and mental, and in the end sent me on a course of fingerprinting. From this I emerged to find myself working for the Federal Bureau of Investigation. It was embarrassing, feeling as I did about J. Edgar Hoover.

However, there were circumstances and things and people to mitigate possible heresy to previous convictions. To start with, there was the Douglas Aircraft plant itself. Beneath an enormous skydrome that might have been inspired by Buckminster Fuller, 40,000 people worked the clock around. From the sky, one could not have told it was there, so brilliant in concept was the camouflage. Or so a test pilot told me.

Driving to work (this time I did not share a lift but used my own car, an elderly Dodge) one approached the drome by a road that appeared to follow the curve of a green, California Hill, up, up past a scatter of small cottages, trees and grazing

cattle. All of this was *trompe l'oeil*. The grass was fibre, an
immense rug laid over chicken wire which in turn covered the
drome. The cottages were forever empty; the cows without life.
Often as I went through the gate under the hill to turn left and
park in the big lot, I wished I could take the white, simulated
road up over tender green slopes to vanish into a Warner
Brothers' sunset. No one would ever know or find me.

Inside that huge, humming confinement we walked along a
wide pavement lined with little plane trees rather like a street
in Paris. And we walked always to music played continuously
as a way of 'lifting our hearts', said the management, and
keeping our minds on our work, supposedly.

My office was a small room flush with the walls of the
building. People talked to me through a hatch and if need be
came in to be fingerprinted, prints being made on the pass that
would allow them entry. Apart from visiting buyers, army and
otherwise, or the odd bigwig, most of the men belonged to the
plant, though my elder brother did push his head through the
window to say he had joined the Air Corps.

'You make 'em, I'll fly 'em,' he said. Mrs. Miniver would
have approved.

As it happened, neither of us seemed fitted to war, despite
our willingness. After almost two years, I failed to live up to
expectations; he, a bomber pilot, hit the side of a mountain
while ferrying a bomber to Australia and, along with his crew,
was killed.

But this came later. Of the two failures, his was undoubtedly
the more honourable, certainly in the eyes of society. My own
failure arose from angry frustration, rather than a failed alti-
metre. Possibly there was a similarity. Mine, however, was a
barometer of delayed social consciousness.

Many of the men who passed through my office and rolled
their fingers on the black ink pad were themselves failures. Old
lags, 4-Fs, concientious objectors. On the wall above my desk
hung a blacklist of 'dangerous characters' apt to sabotage the
plant, like the little slant-eyed men on the Northrop blueprints.

I was supposed to check this list at all times but the entire arrangement seemed to me to be unnecessary. Given the 40,000 odd employees who came and went with the different shifts, it would not have been too difficult to forge a pass and walk into the plant undetected in the crowd of workers. Cops abounded, but could only be in one place at a time.

Other enemies disturbed me. These were in the form of questions to men who came for clearance through the office, questions about their past, their present circumstances, hinting at dangerous potential. I loathed prying. Those who had been to jail certainly did not want to be reminded of it. Reasons for being 4-F or a conscientious objector were, it appeared to me, personal and private. But the FBI prevailed, and I was forced to ask questions.

Maintenance men and riggers made up the bulk of those I had to fingerprint. The riggers were a floating population, mostly big men who got drunk frequently. 'I think I'll tie one on tonight,' they'd say. They were hung about with heavy equipment and jangled as they walked. Their names were poetry and so were the places from which they came. Eurple Dempsey had been on a murder charge and was born five miles south-east of Yukon, Oklahoma. I visualised a spot on the prairie where he had been casually dropped. Sebastian Yingling came from Phantom Hill, Georgia; Syral Christian Anderson from Inverary, Utah; Noah Ploof and Julius Caesar Clopton from Correctionville, Alabama; and many more. Not all were American-born. There was Christian Nygaard from Denmark; Joseph Henri-Pierre Brisard from France; and one whose name I had forgotten from Stromodoloc, Hungary. All these men were scarred, spiritually as well as physically, battered and reticent.

The maintenance men were younger than the riggers, and less inhibited. Among these I had two favourites who were themselves close friends. Both were in their early twenties and seemed to have come together with intent in a world filled with prejudice. Hiawatha Garrett was black, merry and a native of

Shady Grove, Arkansas. I loved him for his optimism and his humour. His friend, Garcia Roybal, was Mexican, classically handsome and quieter than his friend. Seeing them together was a pleasant experience.

Sometimes I escaped into the main building, able to do this because working for Plant Protection entitled me to a green badge. People with green badges could wander anywhere in the plant. In other circumstances I would have been troubled by this kind of hierarchy, but excursions through the immense, pulsating building were worth manifest exploitation.

Passing the lines of welders in goggles and protective headgear, lit up by eruptions of sparks and a hellish red glow, one went on to where aircraft were being assembled. Half-finished fuselages looked like the empty shells of gigantic cicadas. Here and there an engineer's legs showed below the plane's superstructure, like Atlas holding up the world. Voices without bodies were heard throughout other half-constructed craft. I knew these to belong to midgets, hired because they were able to work in small spaces inaccessible to the average physique. The midgets had first come to my attention in the washroom where, lathering my hands, I heard a little voice asking me to pass the soap and looked down to see a miniature human being in a boiler suit smiling up at me.

Beyond the assembly lines was the largest part of the building where planes were put together as wooden mock-ups, scrutinised for structural faults, flimsy as a child's Meccano set, yet looking as though they could fly with the help of large elastic bands. And outside this part of the building was a large area for trial runs, the dominion of the test pilot.

My colleagues never complained when I vanished into the plant's depths for half an hour. Edna, a former librarian, only appeared briefly for the night shift; Phil had no interest in his green badge, wearing it because it was mandatory. He was homosexual and charming, with a fine-edge sense of humour and a passion for jazz. He got on well with everyone, even Murray, our immediate cop who waddled his way through life, hip-heavy with truncheon and pistol, top-heavy with prejudice. This presented him with a dichotomy when faced with his natural good nature. Observing him with Phil I thought that here, at least temporarily, animosity had ceased. They argued about war, disagreeing on its causes. As Phil would say to me, 'It's all profit, kiddo, just profit.'

During my peregrinations I received suspicious, even angry looks and realised other workers probably took me for an 'efficiency expert' checking up on their ability to work. But the plant continued to fascinate me. Goldbricking, as the vernacular had it—shirking or cutting corners—was never my problem. I was as relieved as the rest to clock out and go home, there to forget why we were making so much money.

The months passed. My list of dangerous characters hung unheeded on the wall. Calendar pages were torn off. Far away ghastly battles proliferated and we read about the heroic Marines.

Then, in 1943, these same heroes came to town, rolling in on a great wave of hulking patriotism that seemed to overlook the real horrors most had suffered, those who lived. Incarcerated, we only saw their arrival mentioned in the newspapers; nor did we pay much attention until one day, by their behaviour, they forced their way into our lives.

Gone with the Wind had left a special kind of legacy. The suit worn by Clark Gable was adapted for current wear, and in some circles like those in which Hiawatha and Garcia moved, was know as the Zoot Suit. The jackets were extravagantly long, the trousers pegged at the bottom. They were elegantly flashy and greatly coveted by the young 'hep cats'.

Hiawatha owned one. He told me about it. It was his only suit. They didn't have suits like that in Shady Grove, Arkansas. He owed it to the war. I would have liked to have seen him wearing the suit, but it was reserved for Saturday nights.

On a certain Monday, that summer of 1943, Hiawatha failed to turn up. When I checked Garcia in there was no time for conversation so I asked him to come by later in the day. The five o'clock whistle had gone when he reappeared. I stood watching the swing shift pouring through the street outside my office. Faces looked desperate. Despite the good wages paid by Douglas, people were still too close to the Depression to feel it had actually finished. Thousands were arriving in Los Angeles every day, not just to work at Douglas, but at Lockheed and Northrop and the shipyards. Everyone had money in the bank now, but often no place to sleep. So they slept in their cars.

Garcia's news was alarming. Hiawatha had been beaten up. Who beat him up? Why, the Marines. Garcia was sullen; he was sarcastic; he was bitterly angry. No wonder. The implications of his story were disturbing. There seemed to have been no reason for the attack by a band of Marines other than the fact of Hiawatha's Zoot Suit which appeared to have enflamed them. In fact, Garcia said, they beat up anybody who wasn't in uniform and had a black skin. The police, he said, were there, 'but they didn't do nuthin''. Nothing, that is, until Hiawatha had been crushed. This was simple; they'd found a knife in the pocket of his Zoot jacket and taken him off to jail.

Before Garcia left, I asked him if anything like this had happened before. Yes, it had, though not to anyone he knew. If, then, I asked, Hiawatha had known the danger, why did he wear his Zoot Suit? Wasn't it asking for trouble? Even as I put the question, I anticipated the disgusted answer.

'What if you ain't got another suit for Saturday nights?'

When Hiawatha turned up a few days later, he reported the loss of his pass. He did not look at me as he spoke. His expression reminded me of those other men I fingerprinted. Like them, he was battle-scarred and this had nothing to do with the bruises on his face. The pass, he said, was still in the pocket of his jacket and the jacket was at the police station. They needed it, he said, 'for evidence'. He sure as hell wasn't going back to get it.

As I fingerprinted him in silence, I made up my mind to leave Douglas. I would hand in my card at the end of the week. Everything I was doing seemed meaningless. What price a social conscience when it is proved worthless in time of war?

The Marines would maraud and stay heroes. Hiawatha and Garcia and the rest would search the false green hillside for structural weakness, mend the holes and breakages to prevent the whole great simulated landscape from collapsing, like the camouflage we had built around society. I almost revealed my thoughts to Phil but stopped in time. He would understand, but would refuse to comment. To him comment in times like these was futile. Instead, I simply told him of my plan to leave. He nodded, hummed a bar of jazz, then pointed to the blacklist. And that?

Leave it for my successor, I said, not caring. Let the saboteurs infiltrate the building, sleep in the cicada shells, mingle with the workers in the canteen, talk to Murray who wouldn't know a saboteur if he saw one.

As I parked my car in front of our house that evening, Mr. Rosenzweig came down the sidewalk and turned into the path of the house next door. Like Hiawatha he did not look at me, and when I called 'Good evening', made no reply.

I like to think it was because he didn't hear me.

The Dark Gods

When Miss Mackie learned a few days after her arrival at the
Hôtel de la Corniche on the Côte D'Azur that D. H. Lawrence
had once stayed there, she felt it to be little short of a miracle.

'Isn't that wonderful! To think...'

The manager, Monsieur Laniel, small, grey-haired and with
a face like a kindly rodent, looked at her in mild surprise. He
had offered the information casually as part of his routine
conversation with English-speaking guests. Miss Mackie's awed
reaction seemed to him excessive.

'My goodness, I never dreamed...'

But of course she could not tell him anything so personal.
Instead, she asked if Lawrence had written any of his books here.
M. Laniel thought not. But then Madame must understand it
had all happened before his time.

He watched her as she walked across the terrace, spare,
somewhat youthful for her age, which he knew from her passport to be fifty-six, the white terrycloth robe she wore covering
her to a respectable length below the knees. For some reason
he thought about a poodle belonging to his mistress. Miss
Mackie had the same suggestion of suppressed hysteria, the
same quality of irritating appeal.

At the steps leading to the road below, she turned and waved
her beachbag. M. Laniel waved back. Miss Mackie, satisfied
by his friendliness, set off down a macadam road that ran along
the sea's edge. It was still too early for the swarms of motor
scooters which descended each day like huge, noisy insects, and
the small harbour sparkled peacefully in the sun. Near the sea
wall, two fishermen were spreading coarse nets and Miss Mackie
stopped to watch. The sight was just another of many that had

filled her with delight since her arrival. To her, the little town, commercialised, packed with French bourgeois families on holiday, its nights strident with pop music, explosive Vespa engines and the exhausts of arrogant cars, was still quaint and old-world. She thought how lucky she had been to find it.

And now—she hugged the thought to her and forgot the fishermen—there was Lawrence.

Walking on, she felt the heat of the road through her new espadrilles, bought yesterday at a local shop. A smell of sewage assailed her nostrils, and she grimaced. At least *her* beach was at a considerable distance from the unsavoury stretch of seafront. All the same she would not go very far out into the water. One never knew what one might find.

She had discovered the beach on her first morning. It was unwelcomingly rocky and for this reason few people used it, preferring the open sands south of the town. But Miss Mackie had staked out a small claim on a circular spot of soft, white sand between two boulders. Beyond was a rockpool where seaweed stirred in the clear, green water. She paddled there, lowering her thin body in its modest bathing suit into the cool sea, her head held high so as not to wet her grey curls. Sometimes, she would be joined by two children, such sweet things they were, though they only spoke French.

They came with their grandparents, a gross, uninhibited couple with flesh spilling out of brief bathing outfits. The woman, in fact, wore a bikini and when Miss Mackie first saw the fat, elderly body she was shocked by the enormous indignity of it. Mother might have looked like that ... The thought was too indecent to contemplate.

Now she negotiated the sliding pebbles and settled down on her private plot of sand, contentedly opening the large beach-bag containing equipment for the morning: first her new sunhat, then a pair of dark glasses. These last had been very expensive, but Mother had left her a little money. She did not need her brother Joel to tell her she had earned the trip, was, indeed,

free now to admit that she had given the best years of her life
to Mother.

She took off the beachrobe and spread it on the sand. Her
flat, sinewy body was already lightly tanned but she scarcely
glanced at it before stretching out, offering it without vanity to
the sun. Isolated behind the double security of her closed eyes
and the sunglasses, she thought about what M. Laniel had told
her. D. H. Lawrence had stayed here. She knew so little about
him, least of all that he was once a traveller like herself. Imagine
him, standing on the terrace looking at the sailing boats with
their pretty, coloured sails, or talking to the fishermen. It was
almost predestined.

She thought back across—it couldn't really be forty years!—
to the time when she had first heard of Lawrence from her best
friend Eva Swanson. Eva had gone east to school, whereas Miss
Mackie attended the high school in Mesa Springs, Colorado,
where they had both been born. But during the vacations they
would hold long conversations in the sweet summer evenings,
sitting in the swing in the Mackies' garden, talking of *life and
culture* and D. H. Lawrence, always with an ear cocked in case
Mother wanted something.

'He believed we should turn again to the Dark Gods,' Eva
had said. 'You know, Mary-Louise, like the Egyptians and their
gods. He believed in the—uh—*passions*, the *feelings* that give us
a sort of reverence for life.'

Miss Mackie suddenly felt like weeping behind her sunglasses.
At sixteen, those words had illuminated her world. She felt she
understood them. But, oh dear, it had been difficult holding on
to that reverence for life in subsequent years, and it had all
somehow deteriorated into just keeping an open mind.

She rolled over on her stomach, feeling the sun burning
against her back and thought drowsily: I mustn't stay like this.
I'll be peeling for days. Perhaps Lawrence's gods should have
been sun gods. They seemed more appropriate. The strange
thing was, she had scarcely read anything Lawrence had
written. When she asked for *Sons and Lovers* at the public library,

Miss Plenderleith, the librarian, had looked at her in shocked surprise.

'Mary-Louise Mackie! Don't you know we never allow minors to read that man?'

Lawrence's books were kept locked up on a special shelf. Not for several years did a copy of *Women in Love* come Miss Mackie's way, but though she tried to read it, late at night, after Mother was asleep, she found the text strangely foreign and gave up halfway through.

Yet it did not matter. Eva told her about Lawrence, how he had been persecuted and despised, his paintings confiscated. Perhaps he had come to this very beach, forced to leave the country of his birth, had lain in the sun, listening to the voices of children playing. She fell asleep.

Fifteen minutes later, she awoke feeling dizzy. The children were calling to each other, and she smiled. Little sun gods. She turned her head towards the rockpool to look at them. Instead, she found she was staring at the torso of a young man who lay on his face only about four feet away. His brown skin gleamed with oil; the graceful channel of his spinal column joined buttocks round as melons in their brief orange bathing slip. Tiny hairs glinted gold in the sun. She had never been so close to a man's nakedness before.

The moment became static. She was aware of nothing but that young, muscular body. Then indignation came to her support. This was her sand! Couldn't he have found another place, instead of trespassing?

The young man's head swivelled around, showing the black lens of sunglasses. He seemed to be looking at her, but she could not tell if his eyes were open. She sat up, her back to him, smoothing lotion on her reddened arms. It was sticky and mixed with sand and she put the bottle down, wondering why she was bothering about it. A few more days, and her skin would look like leather anyway. She gazed out at the shifting colours of the sea where bright turquoise changed to olive as though clouds were passing. Her spirits sagged and the clouds seemed to spread over the whole bright morning.

She stood up, feeling exposed and shy. Shaking the terrycloth robe free of sand, she quickly put it on, and began collecting her things. It was too hot to stay on the beach any longer; she felt a headache coming. The sensible thing would be to go back to the hotel and take a nice cool shower.

She waved to the children who had seen her and were calling, '*Venez voir, Madame. 'y a un petit poisson—venez voir!*'

Not understanding, she only smiled. Walking away towards the road she did not look back to see if the young man had moved.

After a shower, she slept again, awakening to the sound of voices in the corridor outside her room. They were young, feminine and unmistakably American. Miss Mackie listened with pleasure and surprise. Except for two Englishmen, who sedulously avoided her as well as everyone else, there were no foreigners staying at the Hôtel de la Corniche and the prospect of talking her own language, without the feeling of being only half understood, filled her with happy anticipation.

She dressed quickly and descended to the lobby, deciding on the way to drink an aperitif, a pleasure in which she had not yet dared indulge. Her strange depression had vanished and she felt buoyant and hopeful. An aperitif seemed entirely suitable to her present mood.

Except for Nicole, the barmaid, there was no one in the small bar, and Miss Mackie felt a momentary disappointment which subsided as Nicole, a small, frizzy-haired woman with a broad, peasant's face, smiled and said, '*Bonsoir, Madame.*'

Miss Mackie liked Nicole. With only a sparse understanding of one another's language, their communication was simple and easy nevertheless. Miss Mackie learned that Nicole came from Marseille and had a ten-year-old son to whom she referred as her 'bambino'. In a brave effort to meet the situation, Miss Mackie produced Rodney, her nephew, suppressing the fact that he was fifteen years old. Nicole, mistaking the phrase *petit garçon*, which Miss Mackie searched for in her French-English dictionary, for grandson, began hoarding lumps of sugar wrapped in domino paper as a gift for her new friend's bambino. Miss Mackie, confused but touched, accepted a few whenever they met.

On being consulted, Nicole now suggested that Miss Mackie try a Pernod. She sensed that her client was in a reckless mood and handed the milky-green drink across the counter, a gleam of amusement in her small eyes.

'*Faut faire attention. Is vairy fort.*'

She moved her head from side to side, eyes rolled up in imitation of someone suffering from the effects of too much Pernod.

Miss Mackie giggled and took a sip, rather liking the taste. The two Englishmen entered, paused as they saw her on a bar stool. The elder, a tall man in mournful glasses with a babyish mouth beneath a neat moustache, bowed briefly. The other, younger and more compact, longish brown hair curling at his neck, looked at her furtively, before plucking at his companion's sleeve.

'There isn't time for a drink, Gerald.' He sounded fretful.

Gerald looked at him with resignation and Miss Mackie felt an empathy, as of one member of the older generation to another. But the Englishmen were already walking away, moving purposefully and silently, with almost military precision. She could not help smiling at the quaintness of their drab khaki shorts, Gerald's dropping to skinny knees, and the other man's tighter and higher on powerful thighs. Both wore open-necked shirts and sandals, but while the younger man's feet were bare, his friend wore green socks. How *English* they were.

She tried to convey her amusement to Nicole who leaned with crossed arms on the bar. Mistaking Miss Mackie's opinion to be the same as her own, she shrugged cynically.

'*Que voulez-vous?*' she said and heaved her little pigeon bosom in a deep sign of world weariness.

Two girls walked into the bar. Miss Mackie knew at once

they were American even before they spoke. They were both about nineteen, one small and brunette, the other tall, graceful and very blonde. There was a nostalgic freshness about them which was unmistakable. Miss Mackie watched covertly as they manoeuvred themselves on to the bar stools, consulted together and chose their drinks. The blonde had eyes the same colour as the flax flowers in the fields at home.

Miss Mackie admired the easy manner in which they conducted themselves, as though they had nothing to fear and everything to expect. Their self-confidence aroused a feeling of inferiority in her and she sought refuge in her Pernod, taking a gulp of the drink that turned to fire in her gullet.

The coughing, tearful result served to establish the contact she had hoped for but was too shy to make herself. Soon they were exchanging information about themselves, and Miss Mackie learned the girls were touring the South of France by car, using this town as a base from which to visit Cannes, St. Tropez and Nice. They were voluble and merry, inviting Miss Mackie by their friendliness to share their experiences. The blonde was Caroline, the dark-haired girl Ellen. Miss Mackie's inferiority ebbed and almost vanished when she discovered they could speak only a few words of French. Learning she was alone, they suggested she have dinner with them at a café on the quay instead of eating at the hotel. Miss Mackie accepted with delight, then wondered if they considered her too eager in acceptance.

After dinner, and a mild argument which ended by Miss Mackie paying her share, they joined the ambling throngs on the promenade. Miss Mackie walked protectively close to her young companions, but could not prevent flattering remarks provoked by their attractive looks, in particular, she felt, those of Caroline. A little tipsy from the wine she had drunk, Miss Mackie, after a loud whistle from one admiring young man, felt called upon to explain.

'It's because they're Latin, you know. Hot-blooded. I don't suppose they mean any harm.'

At the far end of the promenade, away from the crowded, popular cafés, they found a quiet little bistro where they stopped for a last drink. The girls ordered more wine, but Miss Mackie took a *citron pressé*. She thought the girls were perhaps drinking more than was good for them, but said nothing, unwilling to appear a spoilsport.

Presently, conversation died and Miss Mackie hoped desperately her companions were not regretting their invitation. It was at this point she saw the two Englishmen approaching.

'Good evening,' she called loudly, startled to hear her own voice.

The two men stopped, the elder one glancing first at his friend, then at the table. Miss Mackie was surprised to note that he seemed frightened.

'Oh, ah, good evening,' he said.

He stood looking at them a little helplessly, but his friend walked on. Obviously the younger man had no desire to contribute to any possible conviviality. Miss Mackie was embarrassed by his bad manners. Conscious the two girls were watching her, she persisted.

'Won't you join us? I know we haven't been formally introduced but we're guests at the same hotel, and, well ...'

The man called Gerald managed a smile, but glanced to where his friend stood waiting.

'It's most kind of you, but ...'

To her horror, Miss Mackie heard herself becoming coyly urgent. 'Now don't stand on ceremony. We'd just love to have you join us. The evening is still young.'

There followed a few static moments during which no one spoke. Then the younger man called, 'Gerald, old boy, we really must get cracking.' Relief smoothed the furrows on Gerald's brow.

'Frightfully nice of you. But you see my friend and I have a prior engagement.'

As they loped off side by side, Miss Mackie stared after them. How rude. At the same time perhaps it was better this way.

To her surprise, Caroline and Ellen were in the grip of some intense, private joke. Or was it because they found the Englishmen comic?

'We'll just try and nab them another time,' she said. 'I thought you might like some male company.'

Once more the girls exchanged a look of secret amusement, leaving Miss Mackie feeling excluded and rather foolish.

'Those green socks,' said Caroline. 'Wild.'

'The other one was pretty.'

'His friend thinks he's pretty too.'

Miss Mackie watched the girls sipping and smoking and from somewhere floated the long-forgotten face of Ned Decker, pink and woeful. Ned had been the cause of a neighbourhood scandal involving a trip to Denver with the Seldomridges' fifteen-year-old son Jim. At the time Miss Mackie's innocence had been mitigated by subsequent revelations from Eva Swanson. She had tried to accept the startling new truths, but it had been difficult, and not until Ned Decker closed his drugstore and moved away did she feel free to think of him without distaste. After that she had forgotten the whole affair. Until now.

How could these two nice, obviously well-brought-up girls talk so glibly of a subject about which they should really be ignorant? It was all this permissive thing which in truth Miss Mackie did not fully understand herself. Mother had not approved of television.

The next day, neither Caroline nor Ellen appeared at breakfast, and Miss Mackie, disappointed, set off for the beach alone.

The young man sat on a towel near her private area. Furious, Miss Mackie ignored him and went off to splash with the two French children in their rock pool. Emerging, she felt better, but kept her back turned to the young man as she dried her legs and arms. But the moment came when she had to look in his direction and found that he was smiling.

'Madame has been enjoying herself,' he said in excellent English. 'I am watching you with the children.'

His voice was calm and friendly. He removed his sunglasses

and she noticed his brown eyes did not waver in their regard. She relaxed, thinking that she had always like people who could look a person straight in the face. Perhaps he was a little foreign for her taste, but his hair was beautifully combed, and this evidence of masculine vanity touched her. Today he wore a loose tan cotton shirt over his brief trunks, and she was able to talk to him without being conscious of the body beneath it.

He told her that he was on holiday from Paris where he worked in a bank. Like her, he had avoided the main beach in order to be private, and when she suggested he might be lonely, shrugged his shoulders and said that being lonely or not lonely was a matter of choice. Miss Mackie decided he must be shy. By now she was beginning to like him and when he suggested they should take an aperitif together, accepted after only a slight hesitation, arising from the fact that she was unsuitably clad.

The young man, who introduced himself as Raoul Denis, pointed out that everyone wore the minimum of clothing at a resort of this kind. It was the accepted thing, he said, and held her robe with a deference which melted the last of her doubts.

As they walked up towards the road above the beach, she saw the two Englishmen sitting in the scanty shade of a large rock. The one called Gerald was still fully clothed, but the younger man had taken off his shirt and his skin was already a painful scarlet. Miss Mackie, feeling oddly secure and happy, looked at them as at old friends. It wasn't as though they were hurting anyone.

Raoul led Miss Mackie to a little bistro in a narrow street behind the hotel. She was enchanted by the ropes of coloured plastic beads hanging over the entrance and walked through them feeling she was embarking on an extraordinary adventure. Her companion ordered them each a glass of *vin du pays* and she tasted and swallowed, and presently was filled with wellbeing. Delighting in the moment and pleased with herself, she listened only vaguely as Raoul talked of his motor scooter. She heard him saying:

'Perhaps Madame or her daughters would like to go for a ride?'

'My daughters!'

'*Oui.* I have seen Madame last night in the café.'

So that was it. He only wanted to meet Caroline and Ellen. She mustered commonsense. Well, naturally. And why not? But her happiness was diminishing.

'They're not my daughters. I'm not married.' He apologised, but she assured him there was no need. 'Of course I'm old enough to be their mother.'

It was a natural mistake, she added forlornly, and anxious not to reveal her disappointment, explained the relationship quickly, overdoing herself in enthusiastic agreement about Caroline's beauty—his preference, she saw, was for Caroline, and she felt a strange jealousy—ending by promising to arrange a meeting.

She finished her wine and excused herself, thanking him for his kindness. As she walked down the street, she fiercely rubbed the hand he had kissed against the rough cloth of her robe.

The girls were not at lunch, and she remembered they had talked of going to Cannes for the day. Hot and restless, she left her room to walk through the little town, climbing into some sweet-scented pinewoods where she lingered until she realised people were looking at her from the terrace of a nearby villa. She trudged on, arriving at a dusty, withered vineyard where she sat down on a small boulder and tried to sort out her feelings against the clamorous, metallic background of insect voices.

Perhaps the hardest thing of all, she thought bleakly, was to keep an open mind about oneself. Her head began to ache, and she stood up, feeling the afternoon and evening stretch out ahead, empty and dull.

The first person she saw as she mounted the steps of the hotel terrace was Caroline, lounging in a chair by the oleanders lining the railing in fat, white tubs. Miss Mackie crossed over to speak to her, but, once seated beside the girl, found it difficult to bring up the subject of Raoul Denis. She studied Caroline cautiously, trying to see her as Raoul might do. Caroline said Ellen had gone to bed; a touch of the sun she thought.

Careful not to appear too eager, Miss Mackie invited the girl to hve dinner with her, that is if Caroline had nothing better to do. They could try another café, the one where the lobster was said to be delicious.

Wearing her best flowered silk two-piece, Miss Mackie waited in the bar that evening chatting happily with Nicole. Caroline appeared ten minutes later. She wore a yellow cotton T-shirt and faded jeans. There was a slogan printed across the T-shirt, but Miss Mackie could not decipher it, and anyway felt distinctly uncomfortable to be staring at Caroline's chest. She refrained from thinking of breasts.

The dinner was excellent, but Miss Mackie scarcely tasted it. She found herself talking as easily as once she had talked to Eva Swanson. Somewhere along the way, she formulated the notion that Caroline was just like a little sister. She listened fondly, the wine she had drunk heating her sensibility, as Caroline talked about herself,—what a drag school was, her parents' house in the Hamptons, the rudeness of French policemen, the new car her father was buying her. The bill for their meal was large, but Miss Mackie paid it gladly, and when Caroline linked arms with her as they strolled along the promenade, felt an intense excitement that took the form of clowning and giggling. She pointed out the various young men who she thought might or might not please the girl until Caroline, embarrassed, tried to draw away. But Miss Mackie refused to relinquish her, and tightly arm in arm, they continued along the promenade until they reached the little café at the deserted far end where they had stopped the night before.

Feeling authoritative and self-confident, Miss Mackie suggested a green Chartreuse. She had never tasted one, but knew somehow it would fit the occasion.

Caroline smoked in silence and Miss Mackie had to suppress saying she thought too many cigarettes were bad for one. Instead she thought how Caroline's hair hung like a shining helmet or a bell around her face. Afraid that the girl was becoming bored she cast about in her mind for something amusing to say. Then a Vespa buzzed out of the night and came to a stop in front of their table on the promenade. The driver was Raoul Denis, immaculate in very clean jeans and a white and red striped T-shirt. His hair gleamed richly in the light.

'*Quelle chance!*' he said, smiling charmingly. 'I have seen you before tonight, that is to say ...'

He was staring at Caroline. Miss Mackie frowned, smiled, introduced them. She felt the evening dissolving into fragments. No time had been fixed; he shouldn't be here. He must have been following them. She watched the pair talking, Caroline rather off-hand, Raoul attentive, but heard little of what they were saying. He had no right, she thought, he had no right. Her wild hope that Caroline might dislike the young man collapsed as the girl said brightly, 'Why, yes, I'd love to.'

Raoul turned to Miss Mackie. 'Madame will not object if I escort her friend to the Casino?'

His self-assured smile, precluding refusal, his confident male arrogance, aroused hatred in Miss Mackie. Slowly, part of her mind stunned by the words, she said, 'Yes, I do object.'

Caroline looked at her incredulously. 'But Miss Mackie, you ...'

Simultaneously Raoul said, '*Mais*, Madame ...'

They broke into laughter, and in the sound, carefree and youthful, Miss Mackie detected a bond already established.

'From what I hear, the Casino is not the sort of place a young girl should visit.' Her voice was shaking.

'If I may explain,' said Raoul equably, 'the Casino is not what Madame would think. It is *très respectable*—a little dancing, a little gambling—everyone goes there. Surely, Madame does not think ...'

He was being so polite, so reasonable. It made him even more detestable to Miss Mackie.

'I don't think she should go.'

To her dismay, Caroline was on her feet. 'If you don't mind me saying, Miss Mackie, I really don't think it is any of your business.'

'But you had dinner with me.'

Caroline looked embarrassed. 'Yes, and I am very grateful, it was very kind of you.'

Raoul said with conscious, hateful charm, 'Madame understands, surely. One is *en vacance*, one is young...'

'You really shouldn't worry about me, Miss Mackie.'

Caroline was already standing by the Vespa, one hand resting on the seat. Miss Mackie walked up to her.

'I'm your friend, Caroline. You can't just go off like this— besides you don't know anything about him.'

Keeping it light, Raoul said, 'I am *bien elevé*, Madame—what you say, good boy.'

Miss Mackie did not look at him. Once aboard that small, boisterous machine, she would vanish as swiftly as she had appeared. Miss Mackie moved closer, offended by the girl's slight movement of retreat.

'Caroline, I forbid you!'

The words were Mother's dredged up from some corner of her mind where she kept the buried, discarded moments of her life.

Caroline smiled nervously. 'Well, really, Miss Mackie.'

She glanced at Raoul, whose understanding lift of shoulders destroyed the last of Miss Mackie's control. She raised her hand, intending to slap Caroline's pretty, mocking face, slap and slap, hurt her, scratch her, kiss her—oh, God!

Instead, she hit out at Raoul, who sidestepped.

'*Ça, alors*,' he said, and his face was dark with anger.

He looked Miss Mackie up and down, his eyes calculating and hostile, his smile knowing.

'Madame, it seems, does not like men,' he said with malicious amusement. 'On the other hand, young women...'

'Oh, do let's go,' interrupted Caroline, not looking at Miss Mackie.

The Vespa coughed into life and sped off into the darkness, leaving Miss Mackie to stare after it until the noise faded into the distant murmur of the crowded streets beyond. She did not move until behind her she heard the waiter saying something and turned to see he was holding out the bill for their unfinished drinks.

She put money in his hand, walking blindly away. She would never remember anything about her return through the raucous streets, only her arrival at the hotel where she walked straight to the desk and told the night clerk she would be leaving in the morning by the first train to Paris.

After a night of little sleep, she was up and packed before full daylight, deciding to skip breakfast. There would be time for that on the train. As she paid her bill, the Englishmen passed her on their way to the dining room and Gerald bobbed his head in greeting.

On the train, Miss Mackie checked her handbag to make sure of tickets, wallet and passport. At the bottom, she came across some domino-wrapped sugar lumps that Nicole had given her, and for a moment she thought of throwing them out through the lowered window. Instead, she tucked them back into her bag thinking wearily that somewhere in the future she would find a child to give them to.

Mrs Hassett's Holiday

The Channel steamer was nearly an hour out of Dieppe before Mrs. Hassett noticed the tall, young American in the wind breaker. One of the first passengers aboard, she had hurried to the top deck, establishing herself on one end of a bench near the railing, feet resting on her suitcase, a rug over her knees, her small, respectable hat ('for the youthful forties', the shop assistant had said) anchored to grey curls by a scarf. Beside her on the bench, she placed a canvas bag containing her few purchases in France, all ready for the customs' inspector. Not that she had anything of importance to declare—she couldn't afford to buy expensive presents for her family, much less for herself! She pushed the bag further along the bench. Its presence might give people the impression someone else was coming back at any moment. It was a small strategy she frequently employed on trains. So helpful really, now that one could no longer afford to travel first class.

Having achieved her objective, a faint look of satisfaction showed briefly on her still pretty, but fretful face. How right she had been to avoid the crowded rooms below where most of the other passengers had gathered wanly for what was to be undeniably a rough crossing. It was humiliating enough to be forced, simply because one did not have enough money, to travel this long route instead of flying. Even second class via Calais and Dover would have been preferable; one could at least have been certain of a good cup of tea. She sighed, trying to comfort herself with the memory of her doctor's words, 'My dear lady, we are all members of the new poor.'

She repeated the phrase to herself thoughtfully, finding it reassuring because it offered her an approved place in society where she would not be alone with her chief grievance.

A thickset man, black-bearded and carrying a knapsack on his back, paused beside her, indecisively eyeing the empty space on the bench. Mrs. Hassett stiffened and her mouth closed firmly in a forbidding expression. Sensing her hostility, the man shrugged his shoulders and moved on while Mrs. Hassett tightened the rug about her knees defensively. A foreigner from the look of him, probably couldn't speak a word of English!

A group of girls, fresh-faced and exuberant, emerged from the cabin, shrieking happily in an alien tongue and Mrs. Hassett's brown eyes rested on them for a disdainful moment as they conversed flirtatiously with a trio of French deck hands. More foreigners! Most likely they were going to London as mothers' helps—or governesses, as they liked to call themselves these days. A fat lot of help they were, and she should know, having employed a series of them. All they wanted to do was to go out dancing every night and pick up coloured men! She turned her head away abruptly to avoid the indifferent gaze of two duffle-coated French boys who glanced momentarily at the vacant part of the bench, then wandered on, their close-cropped heads bobbing in unison as they moved springily on thick, rubber-soled shoes.

The image of her own son and daughter, teenaged and imponderable, flitted across Mrs. Hassett's mind and she felt the old familiar sensation, compounded of anxiety and impatience, which always assailed her when confronted by the problem of her offspring. She supposed she loved them. Of course she loved them!—even when she was most sorely tried by their disobedience, inertia, and ingratitude. Daphne was positively rude, while Michael, after they had scraped and saved to send him to Winchester, announced that on completion of his National Service, he intended to work in an aircraft plant.

Oh, the cruelty of children!—their blind selfishness and disregard of all she attempted to do for them. One should not complain, but she did long for some understanding, some recognition of the heroism with which she performed her tasteless round of duties—waiting in butchers' queues, arguing with milkmen and window cleaners, coping with inefficient char-women and flighty foreign girls. Daily she trailed across the old South Kensington square where she had lived so much of her life, aware of the change behind the handsome façades of its houses. No longer did they contain the nice, familiar people of her youth; now they were broken up into flats and bedsitting rooms, opening their doors uneasily to the entrance and exit of citizens of a half-dozen or more races whom she had been taught to believe inferior. It was this awareness of change which, perhaps above everything else, aroused in Mrs. Hassett a sen-sation of obscure terror, and because she could not understand it, she discovered there was no help to be obtained—either from her family, the larger world beyond, or, least of all, from within herself.

Tears of self-pity burned in her eyes, but she forced them back, committed for always to a life of emotional under-statement.

Definitely, this would not do. Her present feelings resembled far too closely those which had driven her to see the doctor a fortnight ago; overtired, he had said, as though she needed to be told. A change of air would be advisable, somewhere by the sea perhaps. But they could not afford hotels. There was no one with whom she could conveniently stay. Then George, her husband, thought of Aunt Maude in Paris. She could visit Aunt Maude; it would cost her nothing. But the voyage? Fares were so high these days. Not at all, said her knowledgeable friends. She could travel third-class return via Newhaven–Dieppe. It was really quite simple.

'Try and get the old girl to leave you her money,' George had said, seeing her off at Victoria, then giggled as he always did when conscious of saying something a little beyond the permissible.

Mrs. Hassett regarded him coldly. 'Aunt Maude is my mother's sister,' she said. Indisputably, there was a vulgar streak in George.

She mused on her husband for a time, picturing his good natured face, the meticulously brushed, thinning hair, the anxious way in which he observed her when feeling amorous, an expression identical with the one he used when inquiring after an ailing tooth, or a touch of neuralgia.

Mrs. Hassett hurriedly put aside the memory, just as she habitually closed her eyes to the feelings of frustration which beset her after making love with George. The physical part of marriage, she had long ago decided, was after all the least important.

She gazed vacantly out at the grey billows of sea, felt the ship wallow and plunge as it struck a large wave with a force that sent a torrent of water pouring over the bow. Tasting salt on her lips, she remembered a trip to Cornwall she had taken with George years before the war. They'd had a car then, had parked on a cliff's edge to watch the spring tides, their pleasure augmented by the remembrance of the comfortable hotel to which they would return, where tea would be correctly served beside a coal-fire in the lounge. How easy life had been in those days! She gave her head a nostalgic shake and then it was she saw the tall, young American, standing in the cabin doorway, his blond head slightly bent, his hands in his pockets. He appeared to be looking at nothing in particular, his handsome face wearing an expression of amiable indifference. His eyes turned towards Mrs. Hassett and he smiled faintly, forcing her into the realisation that she had been staring with an intensity of feeling which, unfamiliar though it was and tremulous from lack of use, could nevertheless be interpreted as lust.

Instantly she turned her head away, looking into a middle distance, but conscious all the same that the young man had moved away from the doorway and was coming towards her bench. At that moment she knew that, more than anything in the world, she wanted him to sit down beside her. Yet when he paused in front of the bench, her old habit of reticence rose up to battle with the shock of her desire and, without being aware, she answered his look of polite inquiry with an expression amounting to contempt.

'This place is taken.'

He hesitated, looking embarrassed, glanced at the canvas bag and murmured, 'Oh, excuse me,' walking on with big, slouching steps.

Mrs. Hassett did not move, feeling her excitement emptying out in a rush of disappointment and self-hatred. How perfectly frightful! she thought wretchedly, resisting the urge to cover her face with her hands. How could she have had such an idea? It was positively vulgar, especially in someone her age. Of course, he would not want to talk to a woman old enough— well, nearly old enough—to be his mother. It was only natural, and she had behaved quite correctly in sending him away. But dominant in her mind was the fervent hope that he would return. Perhaps she could explain to him somehow that the empty seat would now be at his disposal, that it had been a mistake on her part.

She picked up the canvas bag and shoved it under the bench. Wanting to be furtive, she deliberately disciplined her movements. Why shouldn't she put the bag out of sight? It was really better down where no one might be tempted to steal it. With all these strange people about, one could never tell. She settled back, unaware that she was frowning belligerently. The American was nowhere to be seen.

Three middle-aged women debouched suddenly from the cabin door, clucking like hens, two of them supporting the third like a lumpy bundle of clothing, her face a green mask under her smart hat. Without hesitation, they made straight for Mrs. Hassett's bench, depositing the ailing woman beside her, fussing noisily as they swathed their companion in scarves and blankets and held smelling salts to her nose.

'You don't mind, do you, dear?' The woman who spoke had metallic blonde hair and a shrewdly kind expression which hardened as she noticed the look on Mrs. Hassett's face. 'It won't be for long. I'm getting her a deck chair,' she said, her tone not quite concealing an underlying sharpness.

'I know your sort,' her expression said too plainly, but Mrs. Hassett only answered listlessly, 'Oh, I don't mind.'

She tried to hide her disgust as the seasick woman, lipstick glaring against her pallid skin, laid a hand on Mrs. Hassett's knee, saying weakly, 'Sorry, love.' Then she retched a little and gazed up with swimming eyes at her companions.

'There, there, Ruth, we'll soon have you right as rain up in this fresh air. I'll just fetch the deck chair.'

The blonde woman departed, while the third woman, rotund in a belted coat, a felt hat pulled down over wispy hair, perched on the bench and looked across her prostrate friend at Mrs. Hassett. 'She was just like this on the trip over. If you ask me, she works herself up into such a state beforehand that she can't help being sick, even if the sea was like a millpond. Not that it's any millpond today. Felt a bit funny myself for a while. It must have been that awful milky stuff the French call tea.'

Finding Mrs. Hassett unresponsive, she relapsed into silence, while from time to time the invalid moaned, 'Oh, dear, oh dear.'

The blonde woman returned, looking annoyed. 'Not a deck chair left. Now isn't that the limit?' She spoke crisply, with an air of authority which seemed vaguely familiar. But Mrs. Hassett's faint interest vanished immediately as she caught sight of the American walking slowly up the deck, and she watched as he paused by the railing not far off, stretching his arms and breathing deeply with frank exhibitionism. Disgusting! she thought, and tried without success to fix her attention elsewhere.

'Oh, oh, Mavis!' The rotund woman was staring with candid enjoyment. 'It's that American I told you about, the one I saw in the passport office. Isn't he lovely?'

Mavis, the blonde, nodded. 'Mmm, just like Danny Kaye.'

'No, he's better looking.' It was the sick woman who had spoken and her companions turned to her with cackles of delight.

'Well, would you believe it! She's come round.'

'Just fancy! Our Ruth's going to live after all!'

'I always said Ruth was one for the boys.'

Hearing their laughter, the American looked at them with a friendly interest, grinned with a certain smugness and walked away. Mrs. Hassett, staring after him, realised with a sick feeling that he had identified her with the three women, that he must think of them as friends travelling together. The unfairness of it made her turn her head to regard the others, the hatred she felt revealed on her face. But only Mavis intercepted her look and instantly an expression of hostility appeared in her own eyes.

'Now that Ruth's better, I think I'll sit down. We're over halfway across anyway. If this'—a barely perceptible pause indicated sarcasm—'lady will just move down a bit—'

For a brief moment Mrs. Hassett considered leaving them, but the thought of joining the other close-packed passengers below, burdened by both her rug and suitcase, defeated her. Reluctantly she moved over; the four women sat wedged together in what appeared to be a companionable row.

Ruth, having fully recovered, gave herself a little shake, adjusted her decorative hat and began to fumble in a large, grey plastic bag, at the same time glancing a little shyly in Mrs. Hassett's direction. 'Excuse me a minute, love, while I put in my teeth. There, that's better. Now, all I want is a good cup of tea. None of that French muck. I always say there's nothing like a good cup of tea for what ails you.'

Mrs. Hassett made no reply, having been revolted, not only by the sudden appearance of her neighbour's teeth, but also by the awful accuracy with which they were reinserted.

Ruth, incorrigibly friendly, said, 'Well, it's been a lovely holiday, a real treat, but there's no place like home. You been staying in Paris, love?' Mrs. Hassett nodded curtly. 'Lovely place, Paris. All those old buildings. Too much traffic, though. I—'

Receiving a sharp nudge from the rotund woman, Ruth's voice trailed off; and there was a moment of awkward hiatus which ended by all three women breaking into simultaneous conversation which, as it extended, plainly did not include Mrs. Hassett. Although she had seen the nudge, Mrs. Hassett pretended she had not, despite her feeling of annoyance. Perhaps now they would leave her alone.

She attempted to isolate herself further with plans for arrival. She would be one of the first off ship, just as she had been one of the first aboard. That way she would avoid the rush and undesirable physical contact with all these people. She stared aloofly at the grey billows of the Channel, trying not to hear the chatter of the women beside her as they relived their week in Paris. Snickering like schoolgirls, they talked of the sights they had seen, the food and the Folies Bergère. Something about their voices reminded Mrs. Hassett of her own friends, particularly the men who, when George had gone to Paris on a business trip, chuckled salaciously and teased him about 'those beautiful French girls'.

And what about her own holiday? she thought bitterly—cooped up with Aunt Maude in the overheated, stuffy apartment smelling of apples and age, herself screaming remarks to the nearly stone-deaf old woman who habitually turned off her hearing aid in order to 'save the batteries'? An occasional walk through the Tuileries or along the quays had been the extent of her excitement, for museums bored her and, of course, she dared not enter a restaurant or bar without a male escort. Once she had gone to the local cinema but there had been an embarrassing incident when she had forgotten to tip the usherette, and the memory of her humiliation and the noisy French abuse still lingered in her mind. For a moment she felt something like envy for these women, commonplace and crude though they appeared in her eyes. At least they had enjoyed themselves.

The talk by now had turned to their Paris hotel and as Mrs. Hassett listened to the businesslike discussion of furnishings, prices, and service, she realised where it was she had seen someone like Mavis. It must have been Brighton or Worthing, perhaps Torquay or St. Ives, for as the conversation advanced, she heard that they were all landladies. Landladies on a spree!

How consistent of fate to assign her, through no fault of her own, three such travelling companions!

The American appeared once more, this time accompanied by a girl, and Mrs. Hassett jealously noticed the attentive way he bent his head to listen. The girl was pretty, of course, if one cared for that arty, Chelsea type.

Beside her, Ruth heaved an exaggerated sigh. 'Well, girls, there he goes. Love's young dream. Wish I was twenty years younger.'

'Hark at you, Ruth. It'd have to be thirty at least before he'd look at you.'

At least, Mrs. Hassett agreed to herself spitefully, and then thought with despair how to the young man all middle-aged women, like cats in the dark, must appear identical. Once again he vanished, and this time she did not even follow him in imagination. What was the use? She stared bleakly in front of her, feeling resigned and empty.

'Oh, look, girls! There it is! Home again!' Ruth's loud voice startled Mrs. Hassett. 'Tra-la-la. *There'll be bluebirds over the white cliffs of Dover,*' sang Ruth cheerfully.

'That's not Dover, that's Newhaven.'

'What's the difference? Newhaven, Dover. It's home, isn't it?'

Yes, it was home, thought Mrs. Hassett without enthusiasm. Soon George would be leaving for Victoria to meet her train. She wondered if the children would be there and hoped they would not. She could not answer questions, look happy, talk brightly, when all that lay ahead was the dreary routine of housekeeping, penny-pinching and jostling for a place in line.

'Cheer up, love,' said Ruth suddenly, and Mrs. Hassett, defences momentarily down, looked at her in surprise. Ruth nodded wisely. 'It's always darkest before the dawn. That's what my old man used to say.'

But Mrs. Hassett had by now re-entrenched herself. 'I beg your pardon?' she said stiffly.

'Come along now, girls,' broke in Mavis officiously. 'We'd

better get our luggage together.'

Mrs. Hassett scarcely saw them go, her thoughts fixed on the impending arrival. She began to fold up her rug with careful hands. Anyway, this time she would insist that George take her home in a taxi. But the thought was small comfort. What was a taxi measured against the weight of her hopelessness?

The boat swung around, preparing to berth, its propellers churning desperately. Mrs. Hassett started down the deck, her mouth settling into lines of disdain.

'I think you forgot this.'

She turned sharply, already on the defensive; then her lips opened in an uncertain smile while a wave of blood mounted from her neck to her forehead, frightening in its unexpectedness.

The American stood before her. He was holding out the canvas bag politely, his expression anticipating her thanks. 'It was under the bench.'

Mrs. Hassett's left arm shot out, grasping the bag awkwardly, her fingers touching his on the handle. The contact unnerved her and she drew a quick breath, saying, 'Oh. I'm sorry—I— how kind,' her eyes beseeching him while he stared, caught momentarily in astounded comprehension, his own fair skin flushing under the intensity of her gaze.

But he only said, 'Oh, that's all right.'

Mrs. Hassett jerked the bag away and, turning, walked rapidly towards where the passengers waited to disembark. Her composure had broken completely; she was blind and deaf to the world about her. The humiliation—the awful humiliation of it! Gradually she became conscious that she might be making a spectacle of herself. Rug and bag were dragging uncomfortably; her suitcase pulled at one arm. She set it down, arranging the rug on top, continuing to hold the canvas bag. Her breath was uneven as if she had been running.

'We saw you.' It was Ruth, her porcelain teeth gleaming in a good-natured grin. Her eyes were warm and she was nodding and chuckling in a knowing way. Behind her Mavis and the rotund woman leered amiably.

'He's lovely, isn't he? I don't mind telling you, I'm jealous.'

'Get along with you, Ruth. I said you were old enough to be his mother.'

'Well, and what if I am.'

They were pleased with themselves and with Mrs. Hassett, inviting her with friendly eyes to be one of them.

She drew herself erect, the training and habit of years reasserting themselves. When she spoke her voice was glacial, her eyes blank with hostility so that they frowned and drew back. 'I haven't the slightest idea what you are talking about.'

She pushed past them, her expression closed and forbidding, and disappeared into the crowd.

'Well, isn't that the blooming limit?' said Ruth.

Mavis said with a shrug in her voice, 'I could have told you,' as the gangplank fell into place with a clatter of finality.

The River

As they reached the curve of the river, she knew he was going to say it:

'Sweet Themmes! runne softly, till I end my song,' the apt quotation, always dropped pontifically in the right place at the wrong time. Divorce had not changed him. And we are friends. Like brother and sister, people said, though behind the remark lurked speculation: 'Do they sleep together? Are they thinking of remarrying?'

For the salacious-minded, it was 'No' to both questions.

She looked at him, her former husband. We are both fifty-five. Together we are one hundred and ten years old. The Themmes is no longer sweet. It is the Thames, an olive surge of turgid water, carrying driftwood, defecation, fallen flowers and the odd dead dog; the river, flowing to a polluted sea.

'Mind the mud,' he said, and put his hand under her elbow.

'Should you have Demeter off the leash?'

Demeter, goddess of harvests, Earth Mother. Demeter, fat, black spaniel, named by their son who read Herman Hesse, mythology, Swinburne, Theodore Dreiser, *Le Morte d'Arthur*, *The Egyptian Book of the Dead*, Chinese poetry and Marvel comic books, to name a few. Malory meet Oz; Jack London, this is William Blake.

'You always were a romantic,' she said.

Without looking at her, he said, 'I would have thought it the other way round.'

'No, I'm more practical.'

'Never.'

Did anyone ever know anyone? His hair was still thick, curling on his neck. His French blood became more noticeable with advancing age. He was still attractive, but slouched. I wonder if he resents me because I remind him he is growing older?

'You lost your wallet the first night you took me out to dinner.'

He knew she was going to say that. She liked reminding him of past weaknesses. She is a threat to my new steadiness. But she is still beautiful, though I no longer desire her.

'And you wrote me a sonnet, a love sonnet.'

'Don't remind me.'

'I kept it for ages.'

If only she wouldn't do this, compel his memory, insist on a forcible feeding of emotions. It would not work. He felt irritated.

'The tide is going out,' she said, and pointed.

'No, I think it's coming in.'

'You should know.'

Did he not live by Putney Bridge, watching the river life, reading and drinking wine from the Wine Society which gave a discount? His flat was a series of small rooms at all angles, the result of renovations made by previous tenants. Now he had been in possession for ten years. His mark was upon it. And his stray people filled the rooms, all save the one overlooking the river that he kept for himself. He had always managed to care for himself, though on the surface it seemed otherwise. Eric is so kind, people said. He allows himself to be put upon. The truth was that he enjoyed it. He ordered his strays around much as he had ordered his soldiers in those martial days when he was a captain during the Second World War, stationed in Assam in charge of movement control, watching troop trains and growing his hair long.

'It will soon be the season for the river boats.'

He looked at her with kindly consideration. 'Yes. But not for a few weeks.'

She had always wanted events to transpire quickly, people to react immediately. She herself always over-reacted.

'Pleasure boats. I'm sure they inspired Adam to write that

song. *All the laughter* ... In the chorus, you know. When the
boats disappear round that curve before Roehampton, the
voices come back, and the laughter.'

He knew she was enjoying her comfortable interpretation of
their son's talent.

'It's possible.'

'Possible. Possible. Now you're being sweetly reasonable, as
you always are.'

But he refused to give up his old TV set, even though the
reception flickered and vanished, filled the screen with white
showers of interference, and often died away into darkness,
leaving frustration and thoughts of added expense. He hooked
the aerial to a coathanger and hung the coathanger on the
bookcase behind the set.

'The riverboats and you, you inspired him too. Listen.'

She sang a few lines: '*My father was a lighthouse keeper, saw the
ladies in their gowns* ...'

'My dear Cynthia, I never inspired anyone.'

The old quaver of self-pity, the flip side of arrogance. She
lost interest.

They walked in silence along the riverpath. The spaniel
rushed into the deep spring grass; a barge went down the
Thames. A large, young man, pink thighs trembling, ran purposefully in the opposite direction. Behind him came a rowing
coach on a bicycle. He called through a small megaphone to
rowers pulling at their oars.

'I'm glad Adam never took up rowing.'

'So am I. But running was always his strong point.'

'And to think I never saw him win his cups.'

'But you were there.'

She shook her head, triumphant. 'No. I never went to a single
Sports Day.'

'But why? I'm sure ...'

'No. Your number two wife was always there.'

'What nonsense. Marisa wouldn't have minded.'

That fat-faced Polish woman with her short hair. She minded

everything. Bitterness, bitterness. But it still hurt to remember how she had stayed away to ease the tension generated between mother and step-mother. For Adam's sake. But that's all old hat now. Forget it. Eric married Marisa and I married Ralph. And here we are walking the towpath like old friends. Both divorced again.

'The tide is coming in. You're right.'

A wedding had brought them together. Eric and Cynthia, parents of an only child, a son. A wise, dancing and singing son who flashed around the world on tours, leaving them to imagine his leaps across all the stages, his singing and his smile.

We both created him.

'But I brought him up.'

She said this aloud and he looked at her with his familiar, derisory side-glance, one she had always found annoyingly attractive.

'Indeed you did.'

He was altogether too conciliatory. She felt she must give him dues.

'At least while he was in his formative years.'

He was not paying attention, calling instead to the spaniel. They turned back along the way they had come. It was a blowy, sun-shot day, threatening showers. She had seen a Turner rainbow earlier over Putney Bridge. Brightly coloured, small sailing boats yawed and turned about, moving sedately down the river. Nearing the bridge, they passed barelegged yachtsmen pandering to their craft.

There was nothing to worry about any more where their son was concerned. He was doing well; a star by current standards, by most standards. He sang and composed and tapdanced sometimes in their kitchens. Mostly Eric's. Mine isn't big enough, thought Cynthia. But I don't begrudge him. Not much. She smiled, remembering how equally complacent they were about Adam. We've discussed it often enough. Both of us artists *manqués* invested our 'art' in our son, who has more talent, that's all.

'Are you pleased about the marriage, Eric?'

'Yes. Are you?'

'Yes.'

'You sound doubtful.'

'I don't mean to. I'm sure it will work.'

But surgery has taken place. Time will tell whether it is minor or major. What rubbish. Adam got married; that's all.

Eric was waiting for her.

'Sorry. Thinking always slows me up.'

'Yes. I remember.'

He whistled for the spaniel. 'She'd better go on the lead now. We'll take the bus from Barnes.'

'And leave the river?'

But she followed him along the path that bisected a field adjacent to the towpath. Hadn't she always followed him, through wasteland and into excitement, knowing money would be lost and senses squeezed, but that the end would be fun? Fun had been expensive. Old lesions caused her to frown; the same old groove, the needle scratchy but still sharp.

If I hadn't spent all that money on him, I'd be better off now. *He* spent it; I didn't. He was frightfully good at spending my money. Officer's pension, soon gone; inheritance from my aunt, up the chimney. Parties. Fifty people instead of the twenty invited, and *his* friend Jason helping to wash up, the two of them throwing the dishes at each other, and I sitting there crying. When the crunch came, he walked away.

He was bending to attach the leash to the spaniel's collar. Why can't I hate him? He's hopeless. But there was no man who had ever given her more sexual delight. Don't think of that. Time and distance have made us incompatible.

When he straightened up he noticed her watching him. She's thinking about sex. If it's with me she had better think again. He let the spaniel pull him along. That's all over; there's someone else now. Thoughts moved smoothly along intimate paths. Hired car; traffic to the Midlands; the same parking lot behind the same block of flats; girl's body after mushroom omelette, two bottles of claret and a cigar.

The repetition of it suddenly sickened him.

'Demeter!' The spaniel looked up at his angry tone, puzzled, having done nothing within her range of taboo. He was walking faster, causing Cynthia to trot.

'What's the hurry?'

'I see a bus coming.'

She jogged obediently. She had always deferred to him in matters of locomotion, catching buses, going to the theatre (even though he sometimes forgot the tickets), leaving him the business of working out routes and timetables and diagrams. The actual execution of such things had made him happy. With her, hurrying was a habit because of his need to be right. And when we get on the bus he will pay, and I'll feel guilty and offended all at the same time because I've always had more money than he.

Panting, they reached the bus stop two minutes before the bus. He folded the bulky spaniel in his arms and they took a seat upstairs.

The conductor made noises at the dog, took Eric's pound note, made change and cranked his machine. He was young with long, lumpy hair, rather like the spaniel's.

'Looks like Demeter's brother.'

'Yes. He almost wriggles.'

They had always been comfortable together when acknowledging the absurdities of life. She felt almost loving but patted the spaniel instead.

'Stupid animal. Oh, lovely Demeter.'

His billfold was new. Even after all these years she still expected him to carry the worn one bought in India and thus beloved. He no longer carried small change in a purse, but in his trouser pocket where there would probably be holes.

'Has the fare gone up a lot?'

'Christ, yes. It's murderous.'

'Oh, dear. May I pay my share?'

The old question. In larger matters he would have said 'yes'.

But this was a bus fare. He would never expect her to pay for her bus, just as she'd anticipated. But she heard the sour note in his voice when he said, 'No, no, it's all right.'

She could afford more than a bus fare, of course. Ralph had insisted on settling a lump sum on her because he felt guilty about leaving her. Then he died out in Canada and left everything to her. Everything meant investments and an income. She felt she had earned the money, but was surprised even now, when she thought about it. He must have loved her; money had always meant so much to him. More than sex.

Eric pushed the spaniel's muzzle down as she looked up between his knees. Cynthia could afford more than the fare. She always managed to come out on top. The rent of his flat was overdue. None of those bastards he housed remembered to pay him. Part-time teaching just wasn't enough. He would have to extend his overdraft. Tired old thoughts. He sighed.

'Are things difficult for you just now?'

'No more than usual.' He grinned, trying a light tone. 'I'd like about £200 though.'

There was no harm in asking, though he doubted she would oblige. He even lost interest himself in the notion.

'I don't think I can manage it at the moment.'

He said nothing, having anticipated the refusal. A silence grew between them cold as diamonds, hard, combining all the feelings intrinsic in having or not having money.

She opened her handbag and took out a five pound note, thrusting it at him sideways, not looking.

'If you insist,' he said. 'You know me. I never say no.'

The bus stopped, shook slightly, lumbered on.

'We're so far from the river,' she said, and hoped he could hear the disgust in her voice. But it's only five pounds.

He began to whistle an old jazz tune. He loved jazz. In the cubbyhole at the flat which he had made for himself with desk, radio and books, a retreat from his lodgers, he would switch on a jazz programme and sing along, or blow happy blue notes through his kazoo. Now, a deliberate afterthought, he interrupted his whistling to answer her. He had heard the disgust.

'I thought you'd been this way before. The river's not far. You just can't see it.'

'Why should I have been this way? It's just the accident of the wedding I'm here at all.'

Accident of the wedding. Images returned. Sweet and sour. Bitter and lovely. She's very pretty. He a young prince. Love and kisses and the champagne Eric almost forgot. I remembered the glasses. And what would they have done without me? Because I bought the cake, the kind they wanted. It was all so quick, like a shotgun wedding, only it wasn't. Just Adam's only week off, and they were, they are, so in love. Poor girl. No parents. So it was Eric's flat or my house. More convenient in London, of course. I don't really like her, but I must learn. That's not true; I quite like her. Anyway, it's for Adam to say. They love each other. Really love. But then, what is love? Everyone asks that. Isolated moments of shared tenderness and laughter and sex. Isolated moments. Then loss. Lost lovers, lost husbands, lost sons. Just loss. What dreadful and beautiful things weddings are.

'It was a lovely wedding,' she announced despairingly.

He turned his head to smile at her. 'Yes, it was,' and put his hand briefly on her shoulder.

With his touch came relief. She forgot her fear and his weakness. Forgot exploitation and resentment. It all dropped away as she returned his smile.

'It was so unexpected. Young people don't often marry these days.'

She had made this remark to numerous people already.

'I don't know why they bothered.'

He had said the same thing to a lot of people.

'Oh, Eric, you don't mean that. They're so happy.'

'I suppose they are.' He sat up a bit straighter. 'I think we'll have time for one drink at The Duke before you need leave,' he said busily. His voice assumed a faintly martial timbre. He was controlling troop movements. 'You can get a number 14 bus to King's Cross in good time to catch your train. You're sure you didn't leave anything at the hotel?'

'Yes.'

The train back to her small house in Sawbridgeworth. Back-gammon with the Floyds, and talk of the wedding.

'I might drive down next month,' he said. 'On my way to Birmingham.'

She'll give me lunch.

'Birmingham. Isn't that where Clare lives?'

Try not to be depressed.

'That's right.' He dragged out the last word ironically.

She stared out the window. Why did I ask? I'm not really interested in Clare, or any of his women.

'I suppose you'll hire a car.'

How can he afford it when he owes the rent? It was all so distressingly familiar. He'll want lunch. Why couldn't he have arranged to have the car today, drive her back instead of making her take the train? But that would be asking too much, wouldn't it? She did not even notice he had made no reply.

'This is our stop.'

He manipulated the spaniel down the bus stairs. She followed. They walked down the High Street towards Putney Bridge. When he spoke it was on a tone of maddening resignation. He understood her silence.

'Look, I'm sorry I haven't got the car today. I could have driven you down. But I couldn't know, could I? I mean the wedding happened so quickly, and there was so much to do.'

'I just don't see how you can afford a car.'

'Oh, my mother gave me an early birthday present.'

His mother! Damn his mother, and his aunts, and his girl-friends. That five pounds; he'd had the nerve to take it!

He turned down a narrow sidestreet, a shortcut to the pub. Part of her mind registered her liking for the street which was neat and sweet, and led to the river. She could smell the river. Sounds of traffic here were not so crushing. The rest of her thoughts swirled in anger.

They used the side entrance to the pub, a white building without much grace, save for a big room with long windows overlooking the river. She sat at a table with the spaniel at her feet. I could use a drink, and asked him to bring her a double gin and tonic.

He can pay. He has five pounds, and who knows how much more from his mother and aunts and girl-friends. The room was quite full. Most of the drinkers were young. The men seem fatter than they were when we were young. They have big stomachs. Beer bellies. Automatically she noted that, despite the slouch, Eric had a lean body. As he set the drinks on the table she felt a flash of desire. It frightened her.

Eric sat at ease. He was drinking beer. She had two long swallows of her drink. His hands are still youthful. The windows were open. Late sunshine sparkled the glasses. There was conversation and laughter. Eric was watching someone behind her. She wanted to turn and look, but refrained. Some of the windows were open. They could see the river, full, and touching the banks. Only a narrow road and a strip of pavement separated it from the pub. A boat with an orange sail tilted by; a small motorboat, weighed down by its driver, rushed past, pointing at the sky.

'Shall we drink to Adam and Jean?' Eric held up his glass.

'Yes, let's.'

This was something to understand, to hold on to against the drag of her feelings. They were a pair, Eric and Cynthia, and they had produced a son.

'To Adam and Jean,' they said in pleased unison, and touched their glasses.

They spoke of happiness, Adam's and Jean's, deciding in favour of it. The chances are good; the outlook is fair and mild. Better than ours ever was, she thought.

'Let's have another drink.' She felt the gin sliding comfortably against her nerve-endings. 'Let's get drunk.'

When he left to fetch the drinks she looked over to where he had been staring. Yes, a girl, voluptuous with long, rippling hair. Resentment made her querulous when he returned.

'This drink isn't strong enough.'

'It's a double. You wanted a double, didn't you?'

'Yes, but this isn't a double. They're cheating.'

'Do you want another?'

Because he spoke sarcastically, she nodded yes, and watched as he took out his change and fingered through it ostentatiously. Ha, ha. But she finally said, 'I'll pay. Don't look so pained. Get yourself one too.'

He was also drinking gin now. He shook his head and went off to the bar, leaving her to sip and look across again at the girl with the rippling hair.

She had finished most of her second drink when he came back. The fresh drink was another double. He slid her change across to her, saying nothing.

She drank, feeling quite merry, enough to say: 'She's pretty. I saw you looking.'

'My dear Cynthia, I always look at pretty girls. You ought to remember that.'

'She's rather young.'

'What of it? All your boyfriends are young.'

All my boyfriends. Sean Merryman and his embarrassing motorcycle, wanting a mother and redolent of cricket turf, footballs, boring when the charm of youth wore off. Hugh Brewster, hearty, frequently impotent, eating too much and teaching her to drink too much. A few quick relationships, nothing important, nothing like the kind Eric seemed to have. It's always easier for men, even now, even in these days of women's liberation.

'Eric, have I aged a lot? Do I seem old?'

'Not at all. I was thinking yesterday what a good figure you have, especially in that suede coat.' Pause.

He's going to make some dreadfully qualitative remark. Here it comes, and it will be in the sweetly reasonable vein.

'I must add, however, that it's good despite your age and having had a child.'

She began to laugh. 'Oh, Eric, you're so ridiculous.'
He blinked rapidly, an old tic, one she found endearing.
'I dare say.'
She's getting drunk. It doesn't matter. I won't have one now.
There's a bottle of claret left from yesterday. I don't think
anyone saw it on my desk. He looked at her a trifle anxiously.
The little lies we tell ourselves. I'm pretending to be virtuous,
but the claret is waiting...
'I think perhaps it's time you left.'
'Yes, I suppose so.' She looked intently at the wet ring left
by her empty glass as though it held a glimpse of the future.
It would be nice if, when we leave here together, we were
going home together. But being together means going to bed.
Two strangers, not even understanding each other's bodies.
Nor wanting to. It would be impossible because we once understood so well. I wonder what he is thinking.
Her bus stop was half way across Putney Bridge. They stood
waiting, watching the slow heave of the Thames. Her head
echoed from the alcohol; she felt inert. The only clarity was
peripheral. Noise and movement lay dimmed and muted some-
where beyond. She leaned over the bridge's parapet.
'Look at the swans. How can they survive? The river's so
filthy.'
'They say it's getting cleaner.'
He turned away, looking over the bridge to where her bus
would appear on the High Street.
'*All the laughter*, Eric.'
'What's that?' But he had understood.
'If you can quote poetry, so can I.'
'So you can.'
'Adam's poetry.'
'Yes.'
People are looking. She's talking too loudly.
'Eric, do you think we could live together again?' She was
facing him, her back to the parapet. He turned her round to
the river.

'No, it's too late. And don't let everyone hear.'

'Oh, no one's interested.'

For a minute neither spoke. Eric absently stroked the dog.

'If you want to bring her down when you come next week I can have her until Adam's back.'

'Perhaps I will.'

Get rid of these tears. Open wide the eyes and don't let them fall. Look down again at the river, moving so steadily towards the sea, yet seeming not to move. I'm not moving anywhere, nor is Eric. Here's the bus. Get on but first a kiss for Eric. He has thought of it too. Our faces bump. Goodbye, goodbye, see you next week. The queue is thinning; I'm the last. Goodbye, Demeter.

Take a front seat. Yes, there's one. She sat, tasting the gin, already stale on her lips. After pain, formality. I shall sit very straight and look ahead and try not to think of what it will be like on the train. It would be better if he didn't come.

Eric walked home. The claret is waiting and there's a good documentary on BBC2. He and the dog waited at the crossing as the traffic went noisily by. The light changed and he dragged the unwilling spaniel away from an attractive smell to cross. The hours ahead were abruptly uninviting. I'll probably get drunk. The meeting had been quite successful but he was glad it was over. Better not stop at her house for lunch. He climbed the stairs feeling depressed and dyspeptic. At the third-floor landing he swore and promised himself to tell the caretaker that the tenants in number four had yet again filled their dustbin to overflowing.